I0684847

The Zambezi Chronicles:

Cover of Darkness

(Book III)

by

Dwight Kopp

For Doe

Chapter 1
Village near Kanyemba
Zimbabwe

A fire threw shadows onto swept brown earth around the dancers. Wood smoke rose and mingled with the sweet smell of maize beer and sweat and laughter. Marie managed to borrow a white wedding dress, a custom adopted from the mzungu. Orange light tangled with the sequins she removed from the dress and plaited into her black hair.

Her father contrived to use the school grounds for the wedding ceremony. He was, after all, the principal. The simple thatched school building provided ample space for the women to cook, and its mud walls cooled the beer stored inside.

Marie danced shyly with the other women while her groom watched from the circle of men around them. She didn't know the man well, but he was young and had several cattle and they would be happy. She was sure of it. The man's uncle made arrangements with her father just before the rains and the big flood that killed so many. Somehow the wedding moved forward and they were lucky. Lucky to have survived. Lucky to be getting married. She would make him many sons.

The gods must have favored them. They paid tribute to the ancestors. The medicine man prepared the appropriate charms against curses, assuring her fertility. The only problem had been her father's youngest wife. Marie didn't trust her. Didn't trust her smile. The woman hated sharing the limelight. She wanted the money spent on the wedding. She was never satiated.

Already the woman had poisoned Marie's mother. Or so some said. Marie believed them and hated her for it. Hated her as completely as if she had seen her do it.

Marie's father principal-ed the local school. He ran the local trade

1

in honey, an essential ingredient in the brewing of maize beer. It takes honey to make good strong beer—the kind that ferments in a man's belly until he passes out.

The drummers seemed to be unaffected by the beer. The women danced, and the men sat together in a happy daze, mesmerized by the throbbing rhythm, the dancing women, the flickering flames and the encroaching fog of inebriation. Marie would lay with her husband tonight, but he would not remember.

No matter; he was a good man. Young and strong and virile.

Marie glanced at her father's new wife. The woman wasn't much older than herself and was the only one to make him a son. His first four wives had given seventeen daughters. Her father had enough wealth to offset the shame. One son was something, and she was glad for her father, at least.

Because of the boy child, the new wife wormed her way into the family, capturing her father's interest and turning him. Marie hated to admit this, but it was true. Giving birth to the only son had given the woman an unfair advantage over the other wives. And the new woman was turning her father as certainly as a man turns a bull with the ring in its nose. She flirted and argued and nagged. The new wife had steadily poisoned her father, too. Poisoned his mind.

Marie knew the woman was planning something evil. She could feel the darkness around her.

It began before the boy child. Once Marie followed her into the bush. The woman said she was gathering mushrooms. Mushrooms. Marie felt a prickling in her ears. Some distance from the village, the woman met a man with one eye. Marie turned away when they lay down together. Didn't want to see it. Couldn't watch her father dishonored. She alone knew the boy child was not her father's. She would not speak of it, of course. Besides, why would he believe her? Marie shivered and tried to shake it off.

The lead drummer's rhythm changed subtly and bounced like a stone falling down a hill. It rolled over the other rhythm, fell behind, and caught up again. Then, with perfect synchrony, the drummers and dancers stopped.

Silence descended. The river frogs listened, too, before starting their own song. The sound of fruit bats and night creatures and frogs joined the whisper of banana fronds in a nearby grove.

The new wife slipped from the circle, walked past her father and stepped beyond the reach of firelight.

#

The man with one eye stared from his place beyond the fringe of light. He wanted a smoke.

His men crouched in the bush around him. Each man lay atop his weapon, blocking firelight reflections off the metal surface. They could smell the beer and see the women dancing. One Eye watched his contact among the dancers. She will enjoy this, he thought. She hated the old man. She hated his family.

It was a perfect arrangement; the men were drunk. Just like night fishing. Torches to draw in the fish, nets to gather them up. Simple. Just like this. The bride was a prize, for sure. She stood out from the others like an angel. His contact had told him about her. Young and strong. The old women were worthless.

He counted the women and children all night. No stragglers could get left behind. So far he had been lucky in his work. And thorough. Yes, thorough. He made his own luck. Not a single person escaped his nets. He was a legend. A night terror. The man who made villages disappear.

He cross-checked the count with his men. Forty-three women and children. Twenty-eight old women and men. There were only two categories: those they would take, and those they would kill.

His men fidgeted, squashing fat mosquitoes, and waited.

Finally he nodded. One Eye's men fanned out in seven pairs surrounding the village. They would move in from all sides. One of each pair would advance and the other would watch from the bush for any who might slip past.

The drummers fell silent and the dancing stopped. One Eye's contact left the ring of dancers and walked toward him. The signal.

He flicked the safety off the Uzi, a gift from his sponsors. His men had their positions. On his signal they turned on head lamps and converged on the celebrants. The villagers squinted at lights that seemed to move by themselves.

The lights floated closer. A superstitious shiver passed over the wedding party. An elderly women panicked. The flash of gunfire exploded toward the men and the old. The bride screamed; her father and new husband jerked with the impact of bullets on flesh. A few made the mistake of trying to run.

The bride threw herself over her father, his hands smeared blood over the folds of her dress as he mouthed incomprehensible last words, lips gaping like a landed fish.

The guns stopped. The assailants said nothing, hiding behind bright lights.

One Eye walked among the women and children huddled on the ground, hands over heads. Here and there he opened fire on someone too old for market. Muffled screams followed every round. Blood and spilled maize beer pooled around those who would stay behind.

"See; I have killed you," One Eye spoke. "You are all dead, even if you are still breathing." He pressed the muzzle of his weapon against every head. Not shooting. Just talking. He let his words

4

mingle with the sound of those still dying. "I own the air you breathe. I give this to you now, for a while. But it is mine, and if you resist, I will take it away. From now on, you belong to me."

Chapter 2
Southern Italy

Ciro Michi lounged in a gold brocade wingback chair praying the Rosary. At least he was trying. Usually it helped him relax.

A soft burbling ring tone announced an incoming call. He picked it up from the humidor cabinet next to him and stared at the number. Good, he thought, finally. He opened the phone.

"Tell me what I want to hear, Lanzo." Michi spoke softly, listening with his eyes closed.

Library shelves and paneling fashioned from Brazilian teak encased thousands of ancient volumes. Red and brown leather books with gold filigree. A rolling ladder leaned on a polished brass rail running the room's perimeter. A domed ceiling supported a reproduction of Michelangelo's work in the Sistine Chapel. Light reflecting on the cherry floor came from a pair of windows framing the French doors. Outside a brick patio shaded by Cyprus wood pergolas incorporated hints of Japanese architecture into the gardens around Michi's Italian manor.

Michi's fingers stopped twirling the beads.

He sighed. "Good."

The phone snapped shut and Michi set the phone and Rosary on the table. He toyed with the ring on his little finger. The American hit man had succeeded. The stock broker was dead.

He stood and poured himself a drink from the decanter. Maybe it was going to work out after all.

Chapter 3
New York Cemetary

A drear spring hung over the New York cemetery. A break in the press of sub-zero temperatures melted much of the snow and left the ground muddy and brown. The damp wind cut through the mélange of granite crosses, mausoleums, and concrete angels set to guard the dead. Zachary Morgan shoved his balled hands into the pockets of a trench coat. He was the last to see Travis before the murder. Travis had given him a lead. They drank beer. They talked a little about marriage. Mostly they talked about the lead.

The report on Sander in the Wall Street journal whirred through Zachary's mind. A drug deal gone bad, they said. Ridiculous, Zachary thought. Travis loved his beer, but drugs? Not likely. But it was New York City; nothing surprised anyone anymore. And no one cared much about the homeless and the stockbrokers. A stockbroker on drugs? No surprise. The case would be left open as a formality, but the police department had enough to do already. Zachary Morgan, investigative reporter, held few illusions any more.

He looked at the deserted cemetery. Travis Sander's ex-wife had not even bothered to show up. Aside from the funeral attendants, he was alone, almost. Another short square man stood at a distance with a black fedora pulled low over his eyes. Travis' mother had early onset Alzheimer's and wouldn't come. His fellow workers from the Brokerage Firm no doubt decided to invoke the Biblical justification, "Let the dead bury the dead". No sense sullying their company's reputation when the New York Stock Exchange opened at the same time every day, regardless of petty concerns like death.

Sander's insurance covered the funeral expenses making it look like someone cared.

Funeral attendants pulled the casket from the black hearse and placed it over nylon cradle straps positioned over the grave. The undertaker looked around for someone to say a few words. He shrugged and pushed a button. Travis Sander's casket slipped beneath the ground like a boat suddenly swamped. The winch didn't make any noise, but efficiently played out the straps supporting the coffin on its final journey.

Zachary felt a knot in his throat. Lives weren't supposed to end this way. Successful people were supposed to grow rich and happy, marry well and end up proud and healthy grandparents or world travelers.

Travis Sander's lead on the culprit behind the massive dam failure in Central Africa was huge. Zachary's story would likely lead to multiple arrests, several convictions and serve up the biggest international story since Rwanda and Burundi. The disaster took the lives of almost five million people. Justice was overdue for the bastard responsible.

But right now, Zachary didn't care about that. Sander's murder left him numb and edgy. He couldn't shake the feeling that Sander's death and the story were connected. It was a time bomb, and he didn't want it to go off while he was sitting on it.

Zachary awkwardly wiped at his eyes and turned away from the hole in the ground. He didn't want to see any more.

Chapter 4
New York, New York

Vinny sat at the kitchen table in his shorts, sweating as he studied the dead man's phone. The old lady on the first floor controlled the thermostat for his apartment. Lucy lived in her bathrobe, wore curlers as a fashion statement, and never went anywhere without a cigarette hanging from the corner of her mouth. Once he asked her to turn down the heat, 'just a bit.' Lucy cursed like a sailor on leave. She spoke to him like she was his mother, which could have been possible.

In the end, Vinny offered her a light and left, giving serious consideration to buying an air conditioner for the winter months.

Vinny stared at the menu options on the phone. The man he murdered carried two. One for business, the other for personal use.

The boss called Vinny after the initial hit. "Vinny. Make sure there are no loose ends."

Vinny saw. Loose ends had to be made dead ends. "I told you boss; it's done," he replied.

"Good. That's what I told them. Make sure I didn't lie, Vinny. I hate to lie. You know that." The boss impressed him with the urgency of the situation.

Urgency made Vinny uncomfortable. When the big man got nervous, something hot was coming down. Vinny had been around long enough to know that when things got hot, usually there was some kind of collateral damage. He didn't want to be collateral damage. Now, his best shot at staying alive was making sure he wasn't the weak link.

"Reading used to be easier." Vinny wiped his forehead on a paper napkin and fished in his pocket for his reading glasses. He pressed the bifocals on his nose and stared at the phone's display.

Recent calls. He scrolled through the recent calls until he was staring at the day before the murder.

Molly, a black and white cat, jumped onto the Formica table top.

"Not now Molly. Daddy's working," Vinny said. The cat began to purred and rubed against Vinny's hand.

"Not now, Molly." Vinny's voice was unconvincing. He selected *Calls Made*.

"This is not good, not good," he said to Molly. Travis Sander had contacted a Zachary Morgan. "I've heard this name before. If I've heard a name before, it is usually not good." Vinny moved to his desk and flicked on his computer. He opened a browser and ran a search for the name with the area code. A picture appeared on screen of a young man with irreverently curly hair.

He had seen him before: the man who attended Sander's funeral.

The photo's caption read, *Zachary Morgan, Reporter, New York Times*.

Vinny held his balding head and groaned. He better get busy. No loose ends.

Chapter 5
LaGuardia International Airport
New York, New York

The Airport snarled with traffic. Zachary Morgan tapped impatiently on the steering wheel. I should have taken the M60 to LeGuardia, he thought, but the prospect of spending his first moments alone with Serena in a bus hadn't impressed him.

He sighed and checked his watch. At last the lane began to move, and he exited off into short-term parking. He had to travel up to the fourth floor to an open spot. Zachary slammed the Ford into park and got out. He checked his wild hair in the dusty reflection of the windows and started off toward the terminal at a trot.

Serena Chavez free-lanced for the past three years, selling her photos to any publication that would take them. Photos seemed to be getting cheaper with the advent of the digital age, but Serena kept her career moving with an artistic flair and a willingness to travel to places other women wouldn't dream of setting foot.

Being a woman had given her access to places men couldn't go. The hidden women of Afghanistan. Victims of the sex trade in Germany. The photographs spoke for themselves, but she could also write, and consequently Serena made more money than he did.

He paused by a row of monitors displaying arrivals and departures on British Airways. Gate E2.

Damn, he thought and set off at a run again. He might just make it.

He stood outside the security gate and waited. The plane, arriving via Heathrow, England, disgorged its passengers into the melee of New York City. "Serena!" Zachary waved her down.

White blouse over faded jeans nicely accented her auburn hair.

11

Always beautiful, he thought.

"Thank God you've made it on time." She smiled and kissed him as he wrapped her up in a long-needed hug.

"I checked your flight information this morning and saw that your plane was ahead of schedule."

In the wake of the Kariba Dam failure in Africa, Serena managed to retain a rogue pilot crazy enough to fly her in and out of places most people would never see. She emailed him enough to hint at the scope of it.

"How was the trip?"

She turned toward him. "Zachary, no one is going to believe it."

Her soft blue eyes seemed tired. Sad. This wasn't one of those trips she could bounce back from with a glass of wine and a long talk.

Serena cared. She cared when she interviewed the refugees from Somalia who couldn't go back for their children. She cared when she heard the stories of imprisoned Christians in Nepal. She cared when she talked to Moslem-Americans about racial hatred and religious stereotyping. That's what made her so good.

"I have the weekend off," Zachary said. "You can crash at my place until I get home from work tomorrow, and then you can tell me all about it." He took her backpack and led her away from the press of people. "Tough trip?" He glanced at her sideways.

"Just crazy. Crazy. Let's get out of here. I need a shower, a scotch, and a bed."

"Coming right up."

She pulled on his hand to stop him. "I'm sorry to hear about Travis."

He looked away, but she put her hand on the side of his face and brought his eyes back to her own. "I wish I had been here for you."

Zachary shrugged. "I didn't see him enough, you know? Once we got busy with our careers it's like we forgot how to be friends."

Chapter 6
NY Hotel Restaurant

Zachary Morgan ran his hands over the stubble on his chin. While Serena was sleeping, he poured over the records in his box. He tucked Serena into bed and willed himself to let her sleep. She was exhausted. The fatigue seemed deeper than jet lag this time. Whatever she witnessed in the flood disaster zone had taken its toll.

He looked out the window of the hotel restaurant. It's about time, he thought. Philip Monroe walked by shifting his sizeable weight from side to side. The man's shoes wore thin on the outside edges, and Zachary imagined the editor's legs chaffed horribly where they rubbed together. As usual, his editor wore a white shirt, gray suit, and black tie. Like a monks robe, same thing every day.

"Why the hell did you pick this place?" Monroe wiped sweat from his face and chin on a white hanky fringed in delicate lace. "I hope they serve a decent primavera." He stuffed the hanky into his suit coat.

"Couldn't tell you," Zachary answered. He wished he had picked a place with more ambient noise. Philip Monroe didn't know the meaning of 'speak softly'.

"So what's with all the cloak and dagger stuff? My office hasn't moved." Monroe picked up the menu and scanned it with a suspicious scowl. "I don't have much time. Better get to the vittles, no?"

"No," Zachary replied. "I'm not eating." The waiter appeared, pen at the ready. "Just black coffee for me."

Monroe scowled at the menu. "In the conspicuous absence of a decent menu," said the editor, "I'll settle for a blue cheese and bacon burger. I want it rare. That means it bleeds a little bit in the middle, okay? Tell the spic in the kitchen I want blood. Tell him to ignore what they said in high school, culinary-arts class about raw meat. I want it red; do you understand?" Monroe waited.

"Of course. One blue cheese and bacon burger."

"Rare." Monroe enunciated the word carefully with two fingers pressed together in the air as if he were pushing a dot onto the letter *i*.

"Rare." The waiter repeated and made a show of underlining the word on his tablet before closing it.

"I'm not finished."

"Excuse me?"

"I'm not finished." Monroe returned his attention to the menu, and turned it over, still looking for the pasta.

The waiter clicked his pen and reopened the notepad.

"I'll take the steak fries, topped with bacon, goat cheese, deep fried onions and a side of ranch."

The waiter craned his neck sideways trying to read off a menu he had already memorized. "I'm sorry; I don't recall that on our menu."

"It isn't. But you have all the ingredients. I checked. Make up a price. Talk to your manager. Do what you need to do. That is what I want." Monroe shot Zachary an exasperated look while the waiter jotted down the man's request.

"You might as well bring me a double of the black tie mousse cake now, so we can talk without interruption." Monroe said. "And I don't suppose you have any decent red wine?" He winced at the startled look on the man's face and continued, "In that case you can get me a Perrier."

"I'm sorry, sir, we don't carry Perrier."

Monroe rolled his eyes and reached into the pocket of his coat and withdrew a ten-dollar bill. "There's a kiosk just around the corner. Get me two of them."

The waiter stood for a bit, unsure if it were safe to leave. Zachary gave him a discrete nod, and he hustled off.

"Perhaps we could finish the meal at an Italian bistro I know." Philip talked as he unwound the cloth napkin so he could study the silverware for spots.

"No thanks, I think coffee will do me just fine," Zachary said. This wasn't his first meal with the editor, but the man's appetite still amazed him.

"Speak for yourself," Philip replied. "Now, why the secrecy?"

"Just a few days ago, I attended a funeral for a stock broker friend of mine," Zachary began. "He was murdered."

"Sorry to hear that." Phillip was bored.

"Yes, well, just before he died, he gave me a lead. I'll try to condense it." He set his coffee down. "About a month before the Kariba Dam failed in central Africa, Travis gets a call. A customer wants to buy up all the copper shares he can get his hands on. Some emerging copper mines in South America look promising. He wants in, and he wants in big. He wanted South American copper. No exceptions."

Zachary paused while the waiter delivered a plate loaded with cheese fries and another with black tie mousse cake.

"Anyway, the day after the Kariba Dam breaks, copper spikes on international markets. It hasn't stopped climbing. I checked again this morning."

Phillip poured ranch dressing over the fries and scraped the side of onions on top. "So where's the story? Sounds like some guy just got rich. No law against that."

"You're right. The man's shares have already tripled in value. But here's the kicker. If the buyer had purchased Zambian copper, which formerly was a leading world supplier, he would have been ruined. Copper climbed because Kariba failed. The Kariba Dam project provided electricity for the copper mines. No electricity, no copper. And Zambia supplies, or did supply, I should say, a huge portion of the world's copper."

"Some guys have all the luck." Monroe licked dressing off his fat fingers.

"If that is what you want to call it." Zachary tried to be patient. "Look. We have to at least consider the possibility that the man who gets rich after a massive dam failure might have known something about it."

"Sounds like you're grasping. How much did this guy invest?"

"Over $200 million," Zachary said.

Monroe's fork stopped midair. He did the math in his head. "That means it is worth over $600 million now."

Zachary took another sip of coffee and let the number sink in.

"That's a lot of cash." Monroe squinted across the table, clearly jealous.

"That is a lot of cash. But it isn't worth the millions of lives lost when the dam failed."

Monroe lifted his chin and scratched the blotchy red skin on his neck. "I'll tell you what, until this checks out—which I doubt it will because I don't know how you're going to get corroboration – keep it under wraps. We don't want our competition to get wind of this. It will be good for at least a week on the front. Then afterwards, probably several months, depending on how it plays."

Zachary Morgan winced. To hear it immediately reduced to sales quotas bothered him, though the thought of authoring the front page of the *New York Times* wasn't unpleasant.

Monroe took another bite, then asked through the food, "Who is this guy, anyway?" Monroe asked.

"According to my research, the buyer is a poster child for the Italian mafia. Lots of money. Lots of connections. Local authorities let him do what he wants."

Phillip stiffened and eyed him carefully. "Mafia?"

"Yes. His name is Ciro Michi."

The editor shifted his weight uncomfortably in the booth, making the bench seat sigh as more air was expelled from the foam. He stopped eating. For the first time he lowered his voice and whispered, "So you think he blew up the dam?"

"Something like that."

"You're not bullshitting me are you." It was not a question. Monroe let out a long, soundless whistle. "This is fucking huge."

"Bigger," Zachary replied. "I've done my research. I have copies of the sales transactions from the brokerage firm. Travis Sander gave them to me the night he was killed. He had the originals in his safe deposit box. He even told me where he kept the key; I thought he was being paranoid."

"Paper? Really?"

"Travis' company apparently doesn't allow it employees to copy sales data onto portable disks. Something to do with their confidentiality clause. Chances are they deal with some heavy-hitting clients who become very testy about other people knowing their business. Anyway, he still managed to print copies of the sales."

"Okay. It looks like those papers are the only solid piece of evidence you have to go on. Please don't lose them. Remember we can't publish this without something concrete."

"I've already put them in a safe deposit box."

"Anybody else know about this?" Monroe asked.

"Not a soul."

"Keep it that way." Monroe folded his napkin. The waiter arrived with a blue-cheese burger. Monroe stared at his food and shrugged. "Such a pity."

The booth seat complained as Monroe pushed himself out backwards and dropped cash onto the table. He leaned over his plate and pinched together three French fries to take along. "Pay the bill Zach. I have to get back to the office."

Chapter 7
New York City, New York

Philip Monroe rummaged through his desk for the container of antacid tablets. He popped several into his mouth and made a face as he chewed. He hoisted himself from his chair and locked the door.

The newspaper could certainly use a shot in the arm. To be the first hitter in an international scandal would be brilliant. But the mob's involvement made Monroe's hands clammy, and he knew he'd have to shake this one.

He opened his personal cell phone and dialed the pizzeria. His fingers fidgeted with a stray paperclip on his desk. He heard a voice and lurched forward in his chair.

"Yes. Tell the manager that I'd like to reserve a table tonight."

#

One neon letter blinked constantly. Monroe crossed the street and ducked into the narrow pizza shop. An exhaust fan exhaling the hot smell of oil and garlic jutted from the brick wall above the entrance.

He nodded to the waitress. "I have a reservation."

She led him through the mostly empty restaurant into an adjacent dining room where one man sat alone with his back to the door. A tendril of cigarette smoke crawled up from his hand like a Japanese dragon.

Monroe straightened his tie and attempted to tuck his shirt in around the bulges.

"Your party has arrived. Said he had a reservation." The woman retreated, leaving Monroe standing in the stony silence.

The boss might have been in his forties, but the bunches of muscle around his shoulders and under his sleeves spoke of a man who spent more time in the gym than a restaurant.

"What can I do for you, Mr. Newspaper Man?" The man spoke without turning around.

"I've got a story you might be interested in, Lanzo."

The cigarette motioned to a chair.

Monroe spoke. "I've got a reporter who knows something."

Lanzo shrugged, so Monroe continued. "Does the name Ciro Michi mean anything to you? I can stop the story, but the reporter said he was going to put the original files in a safe deposit box. Of course, I don't know where that is." Monroe interrupted the flow of his own nervous babbling. He glanced at the man's face, but didn't see any sign of recognition. Instead, Lanzo finished this cigarette and slowly pulverized the butt into a bronze ash tray before exhaling the last lung-full of smoke. Monroe could feel sweat making his shirt slippery.

Lanzo tapped a box of smokes on the palm of his hand and fished out another. A spark birthed a blue flame over the gold lighter. Monroe waited.

Finally, Lanzo leaned back in his chair and for the first time faced him. Monroe licked a drop of perspiration from off his lip. "How much is it worth to you?"

Lanzo sighed, as if trying to decide if he should waste his time with the editor.

"Two million. We'll send it the usual way."

Monroe thought about haggling, but dropped the idea. Lanzo reached out his hand to seal the deal. His grip tightened like iron.

Monroe didn't have the courage to yank his hand away. He couldn't if he wanted to. Lanzo leaned toward the editor's face and whispered, "Bury it."

Chapter 8
Sorrento, Italy

Firelight played over a stone patio resting on top of a steeply terraced hill.   The balcony off Ciro Michi's summer villa overlooked the sparkling Mediterranean and the Marina Grande where narrow beaches squeezed between the water and the ancient town.   Private fishing boats lined the harbors farther along the coast.   All around Sorrento the citrus trees would soon start blooming. Spring tourist traffic had started to pick up.

A young olive-skinned woman served Michi coffee from a silver tray, but he ignored her.

The phone call ruined his day.   With a reporter involved, things could become complicated.   Even for Michi.

For the first time in years, he wanted to kill someone with his own hands.   At this point, it didn't matter much who it was.   Maybe he would kill the woman.   He couldn't remember her name at the moment.   No, he told himself. She was worth too much money.

Michi sipped the coffee, but didn't taste it.

He would have to hide.   At least until he found out how much the reporter knew.   Michi hated hiding.   Soon enough, the reporter would be dead.

Michi watched the fire and thought.   First, he would have to discredit the reporter in such a way that no one would believe him, even if he had already started talking.   Then Michi would find some kind of leverage. A dark secret. Or a woman. Something to force the man into handing over whatever 'evidence' he had.

Then he could kill him.

Chapter 9
Zachary Morgan's Apartment
New York City

Serena Chavez woke to the sound of traffic from the street and glanced at the clock on Zachary's nightstand. Nine already.

She stretched and looked around. It felt nice to be surrounded by the familiar. His closet door stood open. Inside she could see several pressed shirts recently returned from the cleaners. He favored faded jeans and cable knit sweaters. His closet looked like an L.L. Bean catalog. Okay, maybe a worn-out catalog. He could be a model, she thought. Only he was rougher and more angular than the too-clean gentlemen of Maine. She could smell his cologne on the shirt he had given her to wear to bed. She smiled. She didn't remember him getting up. In fact, she didn't remember much at all. He had put her to bed, kissed her on the cheek, and then it was morning.

Serena turned over and saw a plate set out on the bureau with plastic wrap covering a bagel and cream cheese. A note said orange juice was in the fridge.

She got up, stared down at her legs and exclaimed softly to herself. Definitely time to shave. Some things weren't much of a priority when on assignment. It might be different if Zachary could go along, she mused.

That would be nice.

Serena sighed and ran her fingers through her mussed hair.

She had to get to her own apartment. Her mind felt dull from jet lag. She needed to pick up her mail and email photographs to Jarret Miller. Jarret Miller had once been a love interest but now contented himself as her agent. Decent fellow, she thought. Good at his work and thorough.

Serena nibbled at the bagel and padded off to the kitchen for orange juice. Zach placed a single rose on the kitchen counter with a note inviting her to dinner and instructing her to pack for the weekend.

Pick you up at seven-thirty.

Chapter 10
New York City

Vinny stuffed the pistol into his waistband. He buttoned a pressed green shirt before shouldering the suspenders. He donned his shining black loafers and studied the assembly in the mirror.

"How come you're not going out on a date?" he asked himself. "You look okay for an old guy. No life, eh? The only time you get dressed is to make a hit." He shrugged and turned away.

Zachary Morgan was a hot potato. Reporters were dangerous. He had no proof that Travis Sander's had talked to him. According the man's cell phone, the two had been in touch before, though infrequently. Vinny hated to kill a man for no good reason. Still, the money was good and a man couldn't make a living in the Big Apple selling hotdogs. Especially with all those damn vegans, he thought.

Somehow, he had to find out what the man knew, and he had to do it quickly. The reporter didn't live in the same part of town as his dead friend. I guess Wall Street brokers make more than reporters, Vinny thought. Hell, they make more than I do.

"Thieves," he grumbled aloud.

Vinny grabbed a coat and pulled his apartment door shut as he stepped into the stairway. Now, to get past Lucy, he thought. She has such a nose. The stairs creaked as he descended.

"Where're you going?" Lucy opened her door and stared out through the gap allowed by the chain.

"Out, Lucy. I'm going out," Vinny replied with an exasperated sigh.

"Out where?" she demanded.

"Out to murder someone. What do you think?" Sometimes the truth was safer.

Lucy squinted and blew a lungful of smoke through the corner of her mouth. "Na." She made a frown. "You're too soft. Murderers don't keep cats." She knew about this.

"Okay, Lucy." Vinny kept walking.

"Don't slam the hall door, ya hear?"

"Okay, Lucy." Vinny stepped out into fresh air and shook his head. "Yes, Ma," he mumbled.

#

He arrived at the reporter's apartment after dark. The place looked deserted except for a light in the first floor apartment. Vinny peeked in the window. An old man sat in front of a television. Beside him was an oxygen tank with a clear plastic hose running to his nose. Returning to the rear of the house, Vinny let himself in to the upstairs apartment through the fire escape. The fire escape gave access to a balcony off the living room overlooking an alley behind the house and an open bedroom window. Most old apartments had old windows and old windows never closed all the way.

A jaundiced light from the street lamps helped Vinny find his way around. He started his search with the computer on a roll-top desk. An icon floated on a black monitor. He touched the mouse and the screen came to life. He'd need a password to get in.

Vinny pulled a penlight from his pocket. Sticky notes covered the reporter's desk and clung to the front of the desk shelf. His flashlight illuminated various colors. Some had phone numbers. Others, names of people. Article clippings taped to the desk had corrections marked in red.

Vinny sat down. His foot kicked into the computer tower. His light probed farther underneath the desk. The corner of a shoebox protruded from behind the tower. His gun pinched into his side as he bent over to pull the box onto his lap. He put on a pair of glasses and began to rummage.

The box contained an odd and scattered assortment of notes, not unlike those posted across the reporter's desk. It also included articles and translations of articles from Italian newspapers or periodicals published within the last ten years. Every single one had a single name highlighted in yellow. *Ciro Michi.*

"Bingo," Vinny whispered.

He kept reading. This Michi had quite a rap, but the Italian authorities seemed to keep forgetting where they put the evidence, or letting him off on some technicality or another. Vinny recognized the pattern. Somebody gets paid off or someone has dirt on someone else. A little leverage goes a long way.

He couldn't figure why this Michi guy was so interesting to a *New York Times* reporter. A scary guy, yes. Scary enough to keep grown men awake at night, but that was in Italy. Not that it mattered. His job wasn't to understand. Find the guy. Take him out. And don't get caught, Vinny thought. Vending machine murder. Add the correct change, punch in the number and, everybody's happy.

Everybody except the dead guy, Vinny admitted.

A sound at the door brought him scrambling back to the present. He switched off the light, shoved the box under the desk, and made a dash for the window. The kitchen light came on just as Vinny pulled the sash into place. He gulped in cold night air and beads of sweat stood out on his forehead. Too close, Vinny, he thought. You're getting too old for this shit. He pressed his back against the wall below the window and waited.

He heard Morgan in the apartment. Damn. Vinny thought the reporter would be at work. Damn. After a few minutes the front door of the apartment opened and Morgan left.

Vinny cursed and climbed back in the window. He pulled his phone and dialed a number.

"Lanzo. He's not here, but he's been digging." Vinny listened for a long time to the voice on the other end.

"Okay, boss. If you say so." Vinny shrugged and put the phone away. Someone must be really upset. "Plan B," he said to himself, "Put the guy in the spotlight." Apparently the boss figured the man had already talked. If Morgan got in trouble with the law, it wouldn't matter much what he said. No one believes a criminal.

Vinny hunted around the house to find what he needed. He grabbed an oil lamp from the fireplace mantle and poured its contents over the carpet, soaking the file box of notes. He opened a few windows to adequately ventilate the conflagration.

It only took one match.

He waited a full thirty seconds to make sure the fire would gain a solid foothold. Thankfully, the escape stairs didn't squeak and groan like most. On the ground again, he button his coat with shaky fingers.

Forcing himself to walk slowly, he exited the alley, jaywalked the street, and turned the corner at the end of the block. He could already see a line of smoke rising. Perfect. "Don't you know that arson is a crime, Mr. Morgan?"

Vinny turned and walked away, trying to shrug off the thought of the old man who probably wouldn't make it out alive.

Chapter 11
Conrad Blake Residence
New York

Captain Conrad Blake received the call just before dessert. Tory and Taylor burst into their fifth year with all the chaos and color a couple of boys could muster. Their friends swarmed over the house like a mass of squirming puppies tumbling and running and whining and rallying to start all over again. The chocolate cake promised to be a hit. A fireman's helmet with a big number five frosted in black. A Lego ladder leaned against the side of the hat near a window opening cut into the side. A rescue was near at hand with licorice ropes waiting to douse a fire that would erupt near the five candles pressed into the hat. While every boy in kindergarten talked big about growing up to be firemen, the twins openly boasted that their daddy already was one.

In post 9/11 New York City, firemen were still heroes. Heroes, that is, until they had to leave a birthday party for the inconvenience of another fire.

Conrad looked across at his wife when his pager rang. Lisa gave him the 'how could you leave now' look. It was not helping his image. She worked her way through a knot of mothers talking about the benefits of integrated music and reading programs.

"Why can't you call someone else?" she whispered.

"Tommy is out with a broken hand, you know that." He grabbed the pager off the kitchen counter and looked at the code. "I told dispatch what was on today, and Bernie promised she'd find someone else if it were at all possible."

Lisa smiled, but it said something else. "I'll save you some cake."

"Take lots of video for me, okay?" He reached down and planted a quick kiss on her cheek. Her lips weren't available.

Conrad trotted across the room to tell his boys he'd have to leave. They both made faces they learned from their mother, then ran off to play. Just another interrupted day with dad.

Conrad squealed his tires as he turned onto the road. He wondered what else he could do with his life. He could feel the adrenaline that accompanied an emergency call. The rush. The addiction. He tried to deny that this was why he stayed with the fire company, but there it was.

He parked his Bronco in the spot reserved for captain and hit the ground shouting orders. The EMT was en route. They were waiting for him. Damn, he thought. He should have been at the station.

Conrad pulled on his gear; the truck was already running. He jumped in shotgun, as the radio came to life. Residential fire. Possible entrapment.

By the time they reached the scene, an oily black smoke was curling into the night sky. Lights from other trucks and the neighborhood made it look like an out-of-place movie set.

Once on the ground, Conrad hoisted on a tank and mask, shouting orders to his men. Another truck had run out a hose while two men fought with a jammed hydrant nut. They needed water on the roof now!

Conrad pointed his men to a tanker just pulling in and directed his attention to the burning building. A pair of fighters armed with axes followed him up the front walk. The noise of the inferno engulfed them. They knew that to open a first level door would increase the chimney effect, but it couldn't be helped. Dispatch reported an elderly man still inside.

Conrad stood back while one of his men attacked the door with his axe. The door splintered and reluctantly gave way. Conrad pushed his way inside. He motioned for the others to search the front rooms.

Air from the open door pushed grey smoke out of his way. Conrad shouted for the old man, straining to see through the condensation building up inside his mask. He turned into a rear bedroom. An arm extended across the floor from behind a door. Conrad yelled into his radio but doubted if anyone heard. The noise was deafening. The body on the other side kept the door from opening the whole way. Conrad couldn't squeeze through with his tank.

His mind flashed to the birthday cake. The Lego man reaching out. The little window. The fireman on the ladder.

Conrad shrugged off his tank and forced his way through the opening.

The victim at first appeared to have a runny nose, then Conrad realized it was the melting oxygen tube. It must be hotter than he realized. He had to get him out. Grabbing under the old man's arms, he started to pull.

Chapter 12
Sorrento, Italy

Michael and Antonio backed the delivery vehicle up to the loading dock. It was market day—the only day of the week Sorrento's streets were open to vehicle traffic. The warehouse faced a narrow alley—the relic of a time before delivery vans. Antonio managed to maneuver the vehicle into the loading bay, though not without some colorful Italian.

"This is the place?" Michael double-checked the address on the loading bill. "I thought someone was going to meet us?"

Antonio pulled out his cell phone. "We have to call this number." He pointed to a pencil scrawl across the bottom of the bill.

Michael climbed out of the cab, scraping the door against the brick wall. Antonio rolled his eyes and spoke into the phone. "We are here."

As if on cue, the warehouse doors opened and four men in uniform stood waiting inside. One of the men pulled a key from his pocket and undid the padlock on the truck door.

Michael offered to help, but was waved away. Some customers were picky. He shrugged. What did he care?

He pulled out a cigarette and stood watching. The crates were identical. And heavy. He could tell by the way the truck sat low. Odd, he thought. The boxes weren't that big.

Two men stood guard while the other two lowered the ramp and wheeled pallet jacks onto the truck. Six boxes on each pallet. Four pallets. It took them five minutes to move the load into the darkness of the warehouse.

Michael shrugged again. He pinched off the end of his cigarette to save for later. Time to go.

#

The closed warehouse doors blacked out a square of sunlight. A single incandescent bulb flicked on. Stone columns supported upper floors and cast awkward shadows across a brick and mortar floor. Ciro Michi leaned against one of these columns and watched the loaders arrange his pallets in neat rows next to others already in the storehouse.

Michi hated the idea of going into hiding, but taking the gold with him had been a good idea. Gold made him happy. When his yacht was ready—and that would be soon—he would load it on board and disappear. Even his own bodyguards wouldn't be able to find him.

Chapter 13
New York

Serena's simple emerald dress fit perfectly.

"You look magnificent," Zachary said, trying not to gawk.

"You're late," she replied.

"I know. I had such a hard time deciding on my outfit. You know how men are." He opened the car door for her. "How about I make it up to you with some French cuisine? Then we'll nip over to Harriman State Park where I have a cabin reserved for the weekend. We can bury ourselves there for three days and pretend the world doesn't exist."

"Perfect."

"Yes, you are," he replied before closing the door.

The restaurant, once a Victorian home, had been restored to its original grandeur. Zach imagined the new owner would have to be in business for a long time to pay it down. They entered through a stained glass door and were met by Maurice.

"Ah, Bonjour Monsieur Morgan, I have been expecting you. Your table is ready." He led them through the dimly lit general seating area to an alcove set into a rounded turret. A single table, set for two, occupied the space. Maurice held the chair for Serena and left to get the wine. Light from a crystal chandelier danced over Serena's hair and face and got tangled up in a silver pendant hanging around her neck.

"How did you find this place?" she asked in a whisper.

"I interviewed the owner—a biker gang member—just before he was paroled for good behavior," Zachary replied.

"A French biker? You're kidding, right?"

"I never said he was French. Actually, Maurice is part Navaho. Lived in Colorado most of his life until he made a break for the East, the big city and a life of crime—which as I mentioned didn't work out so well for him."

Serena smiled demurely. "Come on."

"Scout's honor, but they say it's the best French cuisine around." Zachary smiled. "Of course, they don't know he's Navajo. He's been a fan of mine ever since I wrote about his restaurant. Says it put him on the map."

She laughed lightly. Zach fingered the ring in the pocket of his sport coat and grew serious. Why should this be so hard, he wondered?

He didn't know if she was interested in marriage. After all, Serena didn't need a man to take care of her. Her work in freelance photography produced more income than his steady job at the *New York Times*.

"What are you thinking?" she asked.

"Nothing." Zachary lied and churned inwardly. Lies already. What hope was there for a marriage these days? Besides, she spent half her time traveling around the world on assignment.

She looked questioningly at him.

"It's just—I'm not sure where this is all going," he replied. "You and me, I mean."

Serena put down her wine glass and stared at him. Her face was serious, almost pale. She swallowed, "It's my work, isn't it?"

"Not exactly. Yes. And no. I don't know." Zachary stumbled. Not sure how to respond.

"Zachary, I don't want things to change between us."

Zach let the ring drop in his pocket and replied, "I don't either, Serena."

He had suddenly lost his appetite.

Chapter 14
Zachary Morgan's Apartment
New York

The ambulance carrying Captain Conrad Blake sped away from the scene.

Burns made Conrad's face raw and fleshy. The smell of smoke and burnt hair filled the ambulance. The medic, a black man with an afro, cut away the fireman's clothing, fighting against the tough fabric designed to protect him. The assisting emergency medical technician re-adjusted the oxygen mask over his face. She glanced at the readout from the oxygen sensor attached to his forefinger and twisted the dial on the tank. Conrad needed fresh air.

The medic banged on the bulkhead and shouted to the driver. "Turn it up, boss. We've got a critical in here."

The second ambulance, carrying the man Conrad tried to save, followed more slowly. It ran with lights but no siren. The old man died within minutes of the rescue, most of his hair had been singed away and the support stockings he wore to improve circulation melted into his badly burned legs.

#

Officer O'Henry watched the ambulance leave and said a prayer for the fireman. It didn't make sense for a young man to die trying to save an old one, he thought.

Neighbors spilled out onto the street and stood scattered behind fire trucks.

One ventured over to the policeman and asked for a word.

"Look, it ain't none of my business, but the man who rents the upstairs--I don't remember his name-- I seen him run to his car and speed away just a few minutes before the smoke started."

O'Henry looked at the man and withdrew a tiny spiral bound notepad from his breast pocket. "You get the make and model of the car?"

"Ford. He parked in my spot once during a snow storm, and I had to ask him to move it."

"License plate number?"

"What? You think I got one of those photographic memories."

"What is your name, sir?"

"I'd rather not say. Like I says, I don't want to get involved. But what I seen was real enough. Maybe the guy was just late or something," he tried without conviction.

"I'm going to get your name one way or the other. We have a fireman down and an old man who probably won't make it. You really want to make this hard for me?" O'Henry spread his hands in appeal.

"Sorry. Didn't know that. Name's Oswald," he said.

"Oswald what?" The officer coaxed, not in the mood.

"Jerry Oswald."

"What's your address?" The officer wrote down the man's name.

"I live right over there." The man pointed to an apartment across the street.

"I can't see the house number from here, Oswald."

"Number fourteen."

"Okay, Mr. Oswald, what do you know about the old man?"

"His name is Mr. Robins, I think. Almost never comes out of his place. Not in good health, you know. I think Robins was hoping to get rid of the tenant so his daughter and kid could move in and keep house for him." The officer took notes.

A ladder truck extended over the roof where a fireman cut a hole to pour water in from above. Fire fighters set up misters around the blaze to draw off heat and keep the fire from jumping to neighboring houses, but now the blaze was subsiding. O'Henry thanked Oswald and made his way over to a knot of firemen who stood talking near the rear of a tanker.

"That was quite a blaze," he said. "Your man going to be okay?"

They shrugged. "He's got family," one of them replied.

"Anything look fishy in there?" O'Henry had his note pad ready.

The oldest of the young men pulled off his helmet and scratched his head. "Of course, I'm not qualified to say, but it sure looks like someone torched it."

O'Henry returned to his squad car and called it in. As soon as he got back to the office he'd complete a Criminal Complaint and the Affidavit for Probable Cause. Arson was a felony. They didn't have to wait for a warrant. His boss would touch base with the media people and ask them to keep a lid on it until they could pick up the suspect.

Chapter 15
Old Town Alexandria, Virginia

The grand hall of the hotel reeked of money. A cadre of waiters swerved their way through knots of conversation serving caviar, foie gras and table crackers with cream cheese. The bartenders kept busy opening expensive bottles of wine.

The fundraiser had been sponsored by some of the biggest names in American cinema—producers, directors, actors and the politicians who, at least for one night, found themselves passionate about the eradication of ALS; amyotrophic lateral sclerosis. Most knew the sickness by the man who made it famous—Lou Gehrig's disease.

Colette Logan picked the occasion to make initial contact with a certain senator. Officially she was self-employed, but a wealthy Texas oil tycoon had contacted her and asked for help with the senator. Senator Blusek was secretly preparing to make a bid for the White House. The Texas oil man was financing the senator's ride but wanted more leverage.

Colette Logan rented an expansive apartment in Old Town Alexandria, Virginia. For this job she took the name Lakshanya Brookes. The first to honor her Hindu father, the second because it made the first easier to swallow. She was playing the part of a rich and lonely heiress. At least she was *playing* at the heiress part. The rich part was certainly true. Of course, it helped that Colette, now Lakshanya, was beautiful, wealthy and charming. But it also helped that the senator's wife, Rose, had amyotrophic lateral sclerosis.

Tonight, and for as long as it took to get what she needed, Lakshanya Brookes would be a champion for victims of amyotrophic lateral sclerosis.

It had been pathetically simple to worm her way into the senator's inner circle. She befriended, Tray, the man's secretary—a closet gay just out of law school. Several times over the past two weeks, she visited the senator's office, lobbying for ALS research funding. Tonight she would meet the senator himself.

The Texas man didn't want leverage between the man and his wife; he wanted leverage between Senator Blusek and the American people. According to the Texan, people cared little anymore if a single senator had a mistress, so long as she was beautiful and he was candid to the public about the relationship.

But when a man cheated on his dying wife, the populace would revile him.

Colette passed a mirror that stood behind a reflecting pool filled with exotic koi. She had the perfect complexion of a Mediterranean woman with deep brown eyes. The straight black hair was a gift from India, courtesy of her father. Her very white South African mother contributed to soften her skin color, though this hadn't been enough to stave off criticism and bigotry from her mother's white family, but it had set the course of her life.

"Lakshanya, there you are." Tray spied her across the lobby and joined her. "I'm so happy you could make it today. You look ravishing."

"I was at Johns Hopkins today talking to some of the researchers I sponsor, and I always make it a point to stop in to visit the patients with ALS. I met Rose there, you know, but please don't tell the senator."

"I've already told Senator Blusek about your passion for this cause. I'm sure he would like to meet you."

"I'm really not comfortable around celebrities." Lakshanya bit her lower lip.

Tray rolled his eyes in admiration. "You are so modest,

Lakshanya." He turned and scanned the hall for his boss. "He's over there, and he's not a celebrity—though he might think he is."

Senator Blusek stood near a portable stage that had been brought in for the event. A tall, well-built man in his mid-sixties, he wore a black suit with a light blue silk tie. His silver hair was combed neatly back, with no attempt made to hide his distinguished and somewhat prominent forehead.

"He looks busy." Lakshanya pulled back on Tray's arm. "I don't want to interrupt."

Just then the emcee of the event took a cordless microphone to the podium. "Good evening, ladies and gentlemen." He waited until the rounds of conversation fell silent before continuing. "It is indeed an honor to join together this evening for such a noble cause. Our goal is not to raise money but to find a cure for amyotrophic lateral sclerosis. And to do that, we need to raise lots of money." He paused while a ripple of laugher passed through the crowd. "Of course we have some famous people represented here tonight. I know some of you are wondering if I'm talking about you—but if you have to wonder, then I'm probably not." More laughter followed. "I'm going to introduce someone you've probably never met. The young woman who will propose our toast tonight comes from far away places and has her own exotic beauty to prove it." He smiled again. Big white teeth. "She has invested herself—as well as large sums of money—in research for the eradication of ALS. Ladies and gentlemen, please join me in welcoming Lakshanya Brookes."

Lakshanya started walking toward the podium and the senator. All eyes turned to her. She glanced up at him and smiled shyly as she passed. He could hear the sound of silk and smell her perfume.

She glanced behind her as she slowly climbed the stairs to the stage. Lakshanya Brookes definitely had the senator's attention.

Chapter 16
Vinny's Apartment
New York

Molly met Vinny at the door. She purred and rubbed against his pant leg, then trotted toward her food dish. Subtle and effective feline communication.

Vinny removed his coat and cap and hung them on the hook on the back of the door. Spring was supposed to happen sometime, but it seemed hesitant.

"You'll have to wait, Molly. Daddy's working." He pulled out his phone and dialed the number of a contact inside the New York State Police. One of the perks of working for the mob included access to a fairly extensive and impressive list of contacts.

"Detective Stevens? The boss asked me to give you a call." Vinny sank into his sofa. "He needs your help to wrap up a situation."

The man listened on the other end as Vinny explained.

Molly jumped on the sofa beside him.

"Just this evening there was a fire at the apartment of one Zachary Morgan." Vinny said, "You need to drop a tip that someone saw him start that fire."

Vinny waited, listening to the scratch of pen on paper.

"And one more thing, find out if Mr. Morgan has a family or girlfriend."

The detective said something on the other end and Vinny hung up the phone.

"Okay. Molly. Time for supper." Vinny walked toward the kitchen and pulled a half empty bottle of vodka from the cupboard.

Molly meowed again and he paused to feed the cat.

Taking the bottle and a coffee cup, Vinny walked into his bedroom and shut the door behind him. It would never do for the cat to see him drink. Sets a bad example.

He unscrewed the lid, ran his finger around the place on the bottle where he expected to start feeling better and poured a shot into the mug. Putting the glass bottle to his lips he took a hit, wiped the back of his hand across his mouth and squinted as the clear liquid burned his throat. Vinny set the alarm, scowled at the time, and sank onto his bed to get down to the business of getting drunk.

The vodka made a hot place in his middle; it was working already. "Brain, brain, please go away," Vinny sang softly between sips.

Chapter 17
Conrad Blake Residence
New York

The twins had gone to bed, finally crashing from sugar and play. Each slept with a talking dinosaur from Grandma Blake, who knew what boys want for birthdays. Lisa made sure the switches were turned off. It would never do to wake up to the growl of a Tyrannosaurus Rex. The squeak of brakes followed red lights that flashed through the bay windows, traveling oddly across family portraits.

Lisa saw the lights and felt sick even before she heard the car doors close. It wasn't Conrad. She knew that already. Before the men came to the door she remembered the way she had said goodbye. Angry. Resentful. She wished she could take it back.

Lisa opened the door before they could knock. It was Tom and the station chaplain. The air from outside was cold and cut through her housecoat. She shivered.

"Where's Conrad?" she asked simply.

"Lisa. There's been an accident. Why don't you get dressed? We'll run down to the hospital together."

Lisa felt a pounding in her head. "Is he alive?" she asked.

"Yes, but he is pretty bad off. I'll explain as we drive. Stanley will stay with the boys until your mom gets here," Tom said. "She's on her way over."

Lisa hurried into the bedroom to pull on jeans. She swore at a knot in her shoelaces before willing herself to slow down. No. No. No. The word kept repeating itself over and over in her head. This couldn't be happening.

Chapter 18
Harriman State Park, New York

The silence of the cabin had been absolute bliss. Zachary stood in the kitchen in the early morning darkness. He squinted at the coffee pot, trying to see the water level. He didn't want to turn on the light and disturb Serena. The futon bed where Serena slept nestled in a far corner of the great room.

Zach spooned the Ethiopian coffee into the basket and wished—for the fortieth time—he had the courage to ask 'the question.'

The button glowed green and Zachary waited for the brew. He couldn't get her words out of his head. 'I don't ever want things to change between us.'

What did that mean? Why should marriage have to mess things up?

He had so many friends who had tried it. Marriage just seemed to be something that didn't last in the big city. No wonder she was scared.

Zach pulled up a kitchen stool and sat leaning on the counter, smelling the coffee.

Someday, maybe they could leave the city, move to Alaska. Or the Caribbean. It didn't matter really. Just somewhere far away.

He rubbed his face, reached a mug down from a hook under the wall cabinet, and poured himself some coffee. Serena was still sleeping.

Zach turned on his phone for the first time all weekend. One missed message from Philip Monroe from Saturday afternoon. Editor. Boss. Zach dialed the number and went to stand in the bathroom in hopes his voice wouldn't waken Serena.

"Where the hell have you been?" Philip barked as soon as he picked up.

"That is none of your damn business. I have the weekend off, remember?" Zach gave it back with a wry smile.

"Well, that answer isn't going to help you much. The NYPD has been calling here all morning. Apparently you are a pretty popular guy right now. You had better get your ass down to the station and start doing some quick explaining."

"What are you talking about?"

"Turn on your television. If I were you, I'd start looking for a good lawyer. Never hurts to plan ahead, you know?" The line went dead.

Zach left the bathroom and cast about for the remote. He tilted the remote toward the window until he could make out the mute button and turned on the news. After a few minutes he saw something too familiar. A photo of him. He felt a strange zinging sensation in the back of his head, and he flicked on the sound.

The report showed his apartment engulfed in flames and then shifted to a picture of Conrad Blake and a file photo of his neighbor. According to the report, the neighbor died en route to the hospital, and a fireman was in critical condition.

Zach listened, mouth open. "An anonymous caller to the Crime Hotline saw *New York Times* reporter, Zachary Morgan, throw a lighter back through his door as he was leaving. Seconds later the building was engulfed in flames. Police say a neighbor reported Morgan fleeing the scene just before smoke became visible."

The cameras switched back to the fire station. "The NYPD have opened a homicide and arson investigation. According to neighbors, the landlord who passed away had tried to evict the tenant upstairs in hopes that his own daughter would have a place to stay." The talking head continued, "However, Police have been unable to locate Zachary Morgan for questioning. Anyone with information on his whereabouts should contact the anonymous tip hotline."

Zach flipped stations and turned up the volume.

Serena turned over in bed. "What's going on?"

"I have no idea. My apartment burned down. Old man Robins died. They're saying I did it; insinuating I was getting back at Robins for trying to cancel my lease." He tried to keep the shaking out of his voice. Zach ran his fingers through his hair and turned up the volume. Another station ran the same story at the front of local news.

Serena sat up and squinted at the screen.

Zach's phone, still in his hand began to buzz. He looked at the caller ID. Travis Sander.

"Who the hell is this?"

He muted the TV with one hand and pressed the cell phone to his ear. "Who is this?"

"Someone you should talk to." It was a voice he didn't recognize.

"Who are you?" Zachary asked.

"A man should remember to bury his phone with him when he dies. You keeping up on the news?" the voice asked.

"I'm watching. Who are you?" Zachary demanded again.

"The only one who can make it all go away."

"What are you talking about?" Morgan's voice was rising. Serena stared at him from the bed, now fully awake.

"You give me what I want, and I'll turn off the heat," the voice replied.

"What do you want with me?" Zachary asked.

The laughing stopped. "I'm surprised at your ignorance, Mr. Morgan. What I want is everything you have in that safe deposit box."

"Kiss my ass," Zachary spat. "What are you doing with Sander's phone?" Zachary asked. His head was spinning.

"I took it after I killed him," the voice said. "It has a convenient register of people he called."

"You are a sick man."

The voice laughed lightly. "Not sick, just impatient."

"I didn't start any damn fire." Morgan was yelling.

"You have a problem, Mr. Morgan. I'm the only one who knows that. Just look at your caller ID. I'm already dead, so I'm not telling anyone. I want those files, Mr. Morgan." Vinny clicked the end button.

Chapter 19
Piero's Italian Restaurant
Alexandria, Virginia

The restaurant where the senator ate his lunch was a quiet affair with a menu that featured exotic salads and excellent pasta. Lakshanya Brookes knew how to find him. The senator thought his lunch venue was a secret. He preferred to eat without the political falderal which did nothing to improve his appetite, or his digestion.

Lakshanya made her own reservations at the restaurant for a few minutes after the senator was to arrive. She knew he usually ate alone. Lakshanya chose her ensemble carefully. After all, she was playing the part of a family friend, not a seductress. A simple black dress. The suggestions of lace here and there were just enough to catch his eye. For now, she would act completely ignorant of his interest. It was all so pathetically simple.

She stepped into the dimly lit restaurant.

A young woman looked up from the reception counter. "Good afternoon. Do you have a reservation?"

"Yes. For two under the name Brookes," Lakshanya said. "Has the other party arrived?"

"They have not. Would you like to be seated?"

"Please."

"Right this way." Lakshanya followed through the restaurant and past the senator's table. The senator looked up from his plate with a surprised smile.

"Senator Blusek. I didn't expect to see you here," Lakshanya said.

"One of the perks of a big city is being able to find a place to hide from the pressure of politics," he said.

"I'm sorry, is this your party?" the hostess asked, confused.

"No." Lakshanya glanced at her watch and looked back toward the door.

The hostess seated her at a table not far from the senator. Lakshanya settled herself while the hostess brought her a glass of the house wine.

The senator wiped his mouth. "I was moved by your toast to the families of ALS victims, Mrs. Brookes, is it?"

"Oh, no. I'm not married." She wrinkled her nose. "Please call me Lakshanya."

"Laskanta?" The senator tried, unsuccessfully. He was off balance from the beginning.

She laughed lightly. "Never mind, my friends call me Anya. Anyway, I'm sure this has been a trying time for you and your wife."

"It has. According to my sources, you have already met my wife."

Lakshanya smiled demurely. "Tray talks too much."

The senator laughed. "Not really, but he has told me that you were kind enough to visit Rose."

"I try to visit all the ALS patients when I'm at the hospital if I can. It always helps me to put a face on who I'm fighting for."

The senator grew serious. "I don't know how to thank you."

"It is nothing, really."

"Nonsense; it means something to me. You are welcome to visit her anytime." He fidgeted with his napkin before looking up again.

"Lord knows, I—we—could use any support we can get."

Chapter 20
Harriman State Park, New York

Zachary stuffed a plastic grocery bag full of leftover items from the fridge. There wasn't much, but it would have to do.

"What are you doing?" Serena asked

He could hear the fear in her voice.

"I'm onto something. I've got to get out of here. I don't want to put you in danger." He rushed around the room like a man on fire. His mind was racing. He might only have seconds until someone figured out where he was and came knocking. Then it would be too late. "I've stirred up quite a hornet's nest. That last phone call was from Travis Sander's cell phone."

"But he is—"

"Dead. I know. The man who shot him took his phone. Now he's after me."

"Zachary, you should call the police." Serena tried to sound convincing.

"Were you just watching the news?" he asked. "The police think I started that fire. If I let them get me, it will be too late. Then they'll know exactly where I am."

"Who are 'they'?" She got up and began to help him gather his clothing. It lay in piles where they left it the night before.

"The people who destroyed Kariba Dam," he replied bluntly.

"What?" she was confused. "I was there. It was a natural disaster, Zach. I saw it. I have the pictures."

"No, Serena. That's what they want the world to think. Travis Sander's knew. And they killed him because of it. He told me about it the night before he died. Chances are the police can follow me. I'm not going to let them find me. I'm taking the car, and I'll call a cab for you. Go stay at your mom's place. Leave your phone here. It can be tracked."

"Where are you going?"

"Away. I don't know yet." He stuffed the last sock in his backpack and zippered it shut. "If you find anything else of mine, get rid of it. Make it look like I was never here; act like you never knew me. He stopped again and put his hand on her face. "I'll find a way to contact you."

Zachary kissed her. Then he slipped out the door and disappeared into the gray light of morning.

Chapter 21
Old Town Alexandria, Virginia

Lakshanya Brookes put on perfume and the spray tingled. When her phone buzzed, she grabbed the bouquet of flowers. A day at the hospital with the senator, doting on his wife. The woman was getting worse, and the Senator was getting closer.

She pulled her apartment door closed and stepped onto the brick sidewalk. The air chilled her legs under the short spring dress as she walked to the waiting car and the senator's secretary.

She smiled for Tray. "Morning," she said. "I thought you had forgotten to pick me up."

"Never," he replied. Tray watched her legs then closed the door of the Mercedes. He had good taste in wardrobe, Lakshanya mused. Far better than the senator.

"How's Rose doing today?" she asked after he got behind the wheel.

"Not so good, I'm afraid. The senator will be happy to have you along."

Tray handed her hot chai tea. "Here you go."

"You know the way to a woman's heart." She laughed lightly.

They drove out of Old Town and picked up the highway north toward Baltimore city, Johns Hopkins University Hospital, the senator, and his dying wife.

#

Senator Blusek put his reading glasses in their case and leaned against the leather seat as his driver navigated the black Lincoln through traffic. Blusek pulled a Kentucky bourbon single from a wet bar and twisted off the top. He poured it into a plastic cup and downed it.

When he last visited Rose, she was unable to make any gesture of recognition. He had to force himself to talk to her. He tried to remember that she could still hear, see, and feel. But she was a shell of her old self. The laughter, the smiles and the silly way she would sing when no one else was listening was gone. The flesh seemed to be melting off her body and in many ways she already looked like she was dead. He could hardly bring himself to kiss his wife.

Tray told him that Lakshanya Brookes was going to be at the hospital today. She was certainly much easier to look at. She was everything Rose was not. Young. Lovely. Responsive. A smile played on the corners of his mouth at the pleasant recollection of her figure. He hoped to see her more often.

Chapter 22
Perth, Australia

German designer Franz Staudt piloted his masterpiece –the two hundred forty foot *Josie*—out of the harbor. The inaugural voyage of his superyacht had been a dream for almost as long as he could remember. Now his yacht was heading for the prestigious ports of Dubai, and her new owner. In only twelve days his work of genius would slip into harbor and be noticed.

Staudt had worked diligently in secret. His arrival in Dubai would be the grand unveiling. It helped that he already had a buyer, though exactly who it was he didn't know. Most people who purchased yachts of this size preferred to remain anonymous. Staudt didn't mind; it added to the aura and mystique of his craft and gave the yachting magazine writers something to speculate about.

"A work of genius," he muttered. Not the kind of genius that flows from one mind, but a genius that joins the strength of many of the world's best shipbuilders into one unstoppable team. With the help of his friend and designer Kurt Avano, the two contrived to get into Russia's Krylov Shipbuilding Research Institute to test their hull design. The lab in St. Petersburg, if it could be called a lab, was the largest of its kind in the world. After that the SSPA's Dynamic Maritime Lab in Gothenburg, Sweden. The sum total of their research resulted in this beauty.

With a beam of over thirty two feet, the superyacht was just wide enough to support a helipad on the foredeck. But *Josie's* aluminum hull was sleek and fast and could easily travel over four thousand nautical miles without stopping.

Staudt's corporation received final payment weeks ago, when its new owner arranged for pick-up in the United Arab Emirates. A perfect destination for a yacht of this caliber.

Chapter 23
Johns Hopkins Hospital
Baltimore, MD

Lakshanya Brookes hesitated in the doorway before entering the hospital room.

"Good morning, Rose." The light clip of Anya's accent brought a cheer into the sterile environment. She stopped when she saw Senator Blusek. Tray sat uncomfortably in the corner by the window.

"Please come in." The senator brightened when he saw her. "Tray said you might be around."

"Are you sure I'm not imposing?"

"I'm glad you're here." The senator was eager. "Rose is coming home today." His voice held no excitement. "Hospice," he added by way of explanation. "Please stay." The man was scared, Anya noticed. Afraid to watch his wife die.

A discharge nurse walked in and the senator leaned heavily on the counter while the nurse reviewed paperwork.

Lakshanya turned to the senator's wife. "You are looking lovely today," she said. Little lies. Lakshanya pulled up a chair and picked up a faded Lutheran prayer book from the nightstand.

Quietly she began to read to the patient. Rose made no response. Most ALS patients lost everything but their mind and their hearing. It was a horrible way to die. Rose's mouth draped open and the muscles around her face were slack with the disease. She lost her ability to smile when muscles stop responding. The progress of the amyotrophic lateral sclerosis slowed briefly with the Riluzole treatment. For a spell the senator and his wife had held on to hope that they would be among the few who could outlast three years. But then the Riluzole stopped working.

The woman snored even though she was awake. Eyes wide and unblinking. The feeding tube and a ventilator kept her alive.

When the nurse left, the senator turned to her and tried to smile. Tired eyes. "Yes. She is coming home this afternoon. Home care. Hospice. It has all been arranged."

Chapter 24
New York

Zachary drove out of Harriman State Park and headed for the town of Wesley Hills. He turned into the first church he found and drove among parked cars until he spotted a Ford whose make and model was similar to his own car. Finding one was easier than he thought. One of the perks of driving a boring car. Grabbing his screwdriver he removed the license plate from the vehicle before replacing it with his own. He didn't know what he would say if someone saw him. Thankfully, the good people of Wesley Hills were in church. He hoped the new plates would provide a diversion and buy him some extra time.

He parked his car and walked six blocks to the closest bank where he withdrew $300 in cash, the most he could withdraw in a single day from the ATM. He knew his bank account would certainly be watched at some point, but there was nothing to do about that, and he hoped the necessary warrants hadn't yet been secured to dig into his finances. Besides, without cash, he was a sitting duck. He did his best to avoid the camera built into the automatic teller. For the first time in his life, he felt the bite of technology's 'acceptable' privacy violations. Video cameras, electronic bank accounts, and cell phones.

Zachary turned off his phone, got back in the car and headed north on Interstate 87 to Newburgh, New York. Tapping someone's phone was against the law, but using a person's phone to track them down was not. Newer phones had Global Positioning System tracking built in to more easily comply with federal network regulations. Because the tracking equipment cost less than a quarter of a million, he presumed the NYPD didn't even have to wait to purchase the pertinent data files they needed from the cell phone companies. He only hoped the NYPD was too busy to look it up.

He had thought about taking Serena with him and dropping her off at her mom's house, but he didn't want to risk her getting caught too. In truth, he was just running scared and had no time to formulate a plan.

He parked his vehicle along the street in a crowded residential area of Newburg and then hit the sidewalk. Before long his car was going to be a hot potato even with the new plates. He walked several blocks, forcing himself not to run. Just look casual. Then he hailed a cab. Once in the cab, he let loose a flurry of French.

"Hey, you're in America. I only speak American." The driver rolled his eyes.

"Je suis desolé." Zachary apologized, but managed to communicate the urgency of his request to get to a hotel in Danbury, Connecticut, just over the New York border. Quietly, he thanked his college French teacher for being such a pain in the ass.

"Danbury is a long way from here. You got cash?" The driver spoke louder than normal, trying to help the foreigner understand.

Zachary looked at him quizzically.

"Very expensive." The driver said again slowly, rubbing his finger tips together.

"Ah, oui. Pas de problème." Zachary held up some cash to prove his point.

"Cha-ching," the driver said under his breath.

Zachary slipped him a twenty dollar bill and yelled, "Vite, vite!"

Danbury was not the direction he wanted to go, but if he was followed, he wanted them to follow him going the wrong way. They merged with traffic on Interstate 84 and crossed the Hudson River near Mount Saint Mary's College. Zachary settled back in the seat, planning his next move.

The driver ignored him. No sense getting into it with a crazy

French man.

By the time they reached Danbury an hour later, Zachary had worked out the skeleton of a plan. It wasn't much, but it was something. He paid the fare and bid his driver "au revoir".

Zachary stood on the sidewalk outside the hotel until the cab disappeared. He turned and circled back to a strip mall. It hosted a Sports Bar, a women's health club, a dollar store and a cell phone store. He slipped into the latter and purchased two pre-charged cell phones and two $50 dollar phone cards, all in cash. He wrote both numbers on a slip of paper. Then he picked up a padded envelope from a dollar store and addressed one package to Gloria Sage, Serena Chavez's mother. He stuffed one of the two phones inside with the short note, 'wait for my call.' She would have it in Poughkeepsie the next day.

He opened his new phone and called a cab for Serena. Then he dialed the number for a certain Victorian restaurant in The Big Apple. Time to call in a favor.

Chapter 25
Washington, D.C.

Lakshanya Brookes showed up with coffee before the regular secretaries arrived. She checked Tray's calendar the day before to make sure this morning was open.

"Good morning, Senator. I figured you would probably need a pick-me-up." She continued the charade of a woman on a compassionate crusade. "You don't look like you've been sleeping."

The senator's eyes wandered over the woman's tight-fitting black pants. Lakshanya leaned over to put the coffee on his desk and adjust flowers delivered the day before. Once again, she felt his hands on her. Gently. Just a suggestion.

Instead of reacting, she just turned to him, and said, "I wish I could do so much more for you, Senator Blusek."

She moved away. The hook was set.

All she needed was the chance to document the man's advances, and this time, she was going to enlist some help.

Chapter 26
Danbury, Connecticut

Zachary Morgan checked himself into a dingy motel and waited. The past twenty-four hours had been miserable.

He peeked through the heavy curtain to scan the sidewalk. He pulled up his collar and went out into the gray drizzle. Hunching down in a bus stop he pulled out one of the phones purchased the day before. Then he dialed Serena.

"Hello?" She picked up after the second ring.

"Are you okay?"

"Yes."

"Thank God. I'm sorry I didn't call sooner. I had to wait until I knew you had a safe phone."

"Where have you been? I've been worried sick about you. You're all over the news. They make you out to be a real psycho."

"Look, Serena. I'm onto something. It's bigger than I thought and someone found out that I know." What if she didn't believe him? He pushed the thought aside and pressed on. "Serena, someone is trying to kill me or get their hands on what Travis found." Saying it aloud, Zachary realized it sounded completely ridiculous.

Serena didn't say anything for a while. What was she thinking? Trying to decide if she believed him?

"Who exactly are you talking about?" Serena asked.

"The Italian mafia." It sounded surreal, even to him. He took a breath, waiting for her to answer.

"Shit!" It was a whisper.

"Hang tight until I figure out what to do."

Chapter 27
Seychelles Islands, Indian Ocean

The GPS marked their location off the coast of the Seychelles Islands. A drizzle occluded Franz Staudt's view of the ocean from the control suite. The *Josie* continued on at eighteen knots promising maximum efficiency.

Josie handled herself beautifully on the ocean crossing from Perth, Australia. Now Staudt would take her directly north into the Arabian Sea. He had been tempted to go farther west to the Somali coast and dangle his life work in front of the noses of the world's most dangerous pirates. In recent months, piracy off the Somali coast reached an all-time high. Entire crews were murdered or set adrift and oil tankers hijacked and ransomed off to the highest bidder. The pirate trade increased in sophistication and attracted mercenaries from other lands who wanted a chance to live the romance of the barbarian. All this had taken a toll on the sale of yachts. Especially big ones. Under normal circumstances a superyacht was ultra bait, and Franz Staudt knew it.

But Franz Staudt had taken his time refining the *Josie*'s design in the Russian and Swedish shipyards, and it would pay big dividends with future customers. Not only was the long, narrow hull fast enough to pull twenty seven knots, pirates would leave her alone altogether because *Josie's* radar silhouette matched that of a US military vessel.

Chapter 28
Outside Harare, Zimbabwe

Gideon Chipinduka stared at brown earth. The mounds didn't follow the tidy rows of an English cemetery. Here grave diggers shoehorned the dead into place wherever and however they might fit.

A president wasn't supposed to spend time in cemeteries getting his shoes dirty, but Chipinduka wasn't a normal president.

He inherited a country that just might have fallen too far.

Chipinduka stooped down and ran his fingers over an enamel bowl placed as a headstone. The single hole bored through the dish to keep it from being stolen had rusted at the edges. The rust traveled under the enamel showing itself in various cracks.

There were thousands of mounds. And thousands of enamel bowls to mark the dead.

Chipinduka watched the sun sink toward the horizon. The rainy season finished late and his hopes of finding the restart button for his country were beginning to fade. Not only was the economy in shambles, but his people still lived in fear.

And why not? Chipinduka stood and walked farther into the maze of the dead, making mud tracks with his black shoes.

Some people had been weeks without enough food. Chipinduka carefully monitored maize donations from the World Health Organization and the United Nations. If he wasn't careful, the few farmers who did have maize wouldn't be able to sell their crops. After all, why would someone buy maize when it could be had for free? Free maize put many African farmers out of business resulting in increased dependence on outside aid. Chipinduka shook his head. He would not sacrifice the future of his country for a temporary fix. There would always be critics. He had not taken this job to be popular.

But there were other problems, too. Stories that made his skin crawl. Bands of brigands, likely leftovers from the former regime, terrorized outlying areas, rounding up villages and selling them.

It wasn't a new story. Slavers had been moving people out of Africa for hundreds of years following ancient Arab trading routes. Black men selling other black man. But not on this scale; not in recent times. A slavery that exploited the powerless was too much for an already broken country to carry.

For a moment, Gideon felt the white heat of rage. It wasn't just here. Chipinduka heard recent stories of illegal immigrants out of Mexico headed for the United States, rounded-up in groups of fifty or more by bandits. The bandits raped, abused and extorted them, selling them back to their families. If the families couldn't pay, the hostages were killed.

The most vulnerable people were the ones no one was watching.

And no one was watching Zimbabwe.

Chipinduka stopped at a child-sized mound and knelt down. He knew the woman whose hands patted it smooth and wept over the dirt.

Gideon's choked voice came in a whisper. "I am sorry I have failed you, little one."

He must do something to stop the bleeding. Something to give his people reason to believe again.

Why should he ask them to trust him when Zimbabwe's previous government gave them no cause to believe?

Gideon stood and turned toward his car and the man who served as chauffeur and secretary. "I need you to set up an appointment for me."

Chapter 29
Danbury, Connecticut

Maurice, the Navajo-biker-cum-French-chef, sent Zachary to a diner halfway between the train station and hospital on the down side of Danbury. Zachary installed himself in a corner booth to keep an eye on the parking lot.

Franny, the waitress, was a bulging woman on the wrong side of fifty who still dressed in a too-tight mini skirt and talked around a wad of pink bubble gum.

"How do you want your eggs, honey?" She tapped the end of her pen on the order pad. Her vice gravelly from too many cigarettes.

"Over easy would be fine." He handed her the folded menu.

For the last 48 hours Zachary had surfed news channels relentlessly. But aside from one brief mention, a blurb without a picture, the good people of Danbury didn't seem concerned about another fire in the big Apple. Still, Zachary let the stubble grow and avoided eye contact. He was running out of time.

Zachary worried about the fireman. Whoever had Travis Sander's phone played for keeps. Zachary already sent a text to Sander's phone with his new cell number. Not that Zachary wanted to talk to him, but if this guy got pissed off, he could cross the fireman off the list. Right now, he didn't want to lose contact. After all, this guy with the phone just might be the only one who could make this all go away.

Franny slid a plate of over-easy eggs and home fries onto the pitted table.

"You want ketchup, honey?" She set the sticky bottle down without waiting for an answer and refilled his coffee.

A string of motorcycles pulled into the parking lot, making the silverware rattle. The bikers swarmed in by twos and dismounted, leaving their bikes running.

"Oh, here we go." Franny stared out the window at the leather and metal clad men. They continued to fill all the remaining spots in the parking lot. The thunder increased as more filed in. Once all parking slots filled, they began another row behind. Zachary counted forty.

On the last motorcycle sat a fat man with a long, silver grey beard. His tired black jacket had seen years of sun.

As he dismounted and reached for the kill switch on his bike, every other man did the same. It was a marvel of timing. Deafening silence. Not a single fork could be heard in the restaurant. Every patron's face was to the window.

Zachary Morgan tried not to smile.

The big man spat out a brown stream of tobacco juice and leered in the diner windows. Then he pushed through the smeary door making the bell ring.

"Looks like we're just in time for breakfast." He stood in the silence and looked around. "I'm sure you folks won't mind making space for my boys." He glowered at the patrons in the bench seats until, one by one, they got up and left.

The boys began to file in, filling up the diner as completely as they had the parking lot. A few patrons wandered around outside, unsure how to get their trapped vehicles out of the lot.

Zachary Morgan got up and stepped toward the restroom. One of the bikers, carrying a leather pack, followed him in.

Fat Man squeezed into Zachary's table and motioned to Franny, standing frozen by the counter. "Hey, lady. The boys want eggs and coffee. Make it quick. We're on a schedule."

Chapter 30
Poughkeepsie, New York

Serena Chavez stared at the phone in her lap. The last few days had been a blur of television spots about Zachary. None sounded anything like the man she was in love with.

Thankfully, few people knew about their romance. They decided to play it quiet until she got back from Africa. But eventually someone was going to figure out that he was with her the night of the fire. When they did, she would be a suspect or end up wanted by the mafia like he was. Of course, the police might not find out about her. But it wouldn't look good if they did.

Maybe she could call the police now. Explain that Zachary was being framed because he was on to something.

If the police found out Zachary was with her before she called them, she would have no credibility. If she called in now, maybe they would believe her. Maybe.

"What the hell am I thinking?" She paced around her mother's apartment before sitting down again. It would never work. She had nothing. No evidence. No alibi. No boyfriend, for that matter. Where was he, anyway?

She pushed back a tear and tossed the phone onto the coffee table.

Chapter 31
Alexandria, Virginia

Lakshanya Brookes let herself into Tray's apartment where he sat cross-legged on the floor fiddling with an arrangement of glass beads in a miniature Zen garden. Time to bring in her co-conspirator.

"Hello Tray," she spoke softly. The element of surprise.

He was startled, but his face brightened. "How did you get in here?"

"I'm sorry to startle you," she continued to whisper, "I should have knocked, but the door was unlocked."

He looked confused; sure he had locked it himself, then shrugged.

Lakshanya settled on the carpet close to him. "I just really needed to talk to you."

Tray blushed. She could tell he was flattered and shy about his boss's prettiest friend visiting his humble apartment. "Sure. Anytime."

"It's Rose," she began.

"What about Rose?"

Lakshanya could see the fear. He loved the old woman. She probably filled some kind of mother roll in his life.

"She's okay, I guess," she started, "I'm just worried what she is thinking."

"What do you mean?" Tray was confused.

"Well, I know she can't talk anymore, but doctors say her mind is

73

still perfectly healthy. How do you think she feels when she has to watch the senator make passes at me?"

"What are you talking about?" Tray was immediately angry. "He's been touching you in the hospital?"

"It felt so awkward. I just didn't know what to do. I thought you would be able to help me. The senator isn't the kind of man I thought he was."

"What an asshole." Tray stood and began to pace. "I can't believe he would come on to you. And with Rose watching? She was like a mother to me. It is because of her that I got a job with the senator."

Lakshanya reached up and touched his arm. "How do men like that make it into public office?" She paused, acting shy. Uncomfortable. "I want to tell someone, but who would believe me? People love him."

Tray stopped mid-stride. "Let's film him."

"What do you mean?" Lakshanya suppressed the urge to smile. She anticipated having to lead the conversation this direction.

"I mean catch him in the act." He was pacing again. "We'll set up a hidden camera in his office. That should be easy enough. I'm always in there before he is. Then you stop by. If he starts feeling you up, we'll have it on film. Then the bastard won't be able to deny it."

Chapter 32
Harare, Zimbabwe

Stuart Hall handed his papers to the military police officer at the entrance to the presidential compound. It had been a long time since he had seen his friend. Stuart was busy trying to recover his farm from damage caused by the miscreants who kicked him off. He wasn't tall but a life of farm labor squared his back and shoulders. He felt older now. Stuart was, after all, almost sixty. The African sun burned permanent creases into his tanned face and though his hair was still the color of sand, it was thinner now.

The officer cleared him through security. The president was expecting him. Following an armed soldier along a brick pathway lined with carefully manicured shrubs, he ascended the wide marble stairs and saluted another security guard standing at attention beside the front door.

"Is the president inside?" Stuart asked.

"No, sir." The guard gestured with his chin to the garden.

He escorted Stuart around the path to a terraced garden that descended away from the mansion. A gardener knelt, half buried in greenery, wrestling a recalcitrant weed. The soldier nodded and looked at the ground.

"Excuse, me. Where might I find the president?" Stuart eyes squinted in the sun, trying to see over the hedge.

"President of which country?" The voice was familiar.

Stuart grinned. "The big man who lives in this fancy place."

The gardener backed out of the shrubbery. "He is probably busy with the affairs of State."

Stuart crouched next to the man. "Don't you have something more important to do, Gideon, than grovel around on your knees, pulling weeds? Surely you have a gardener?"

President Gideon Chipinduka brushed off his hands. "I can't afford one. Besides," he shook Stuart's hand, "A man who isn't connected to the earth cannot remain connected to his people." Chipinduka chuckled. "They think I'm crazy," he gestured toward the guards, "but when a man has spent so much time in prison, he does not want to spend the rest of his life caged in a room."

Stuart smiled. "This is true." They got up and started to walk together. "I heard you wanted to see me?" Stuart said.

Gideon Chipinduka's face turned serious. "Yes. Thank you for coming. I need to speak with you—one of the fathers of our country." He turned to the guard. "It is ok. This man is my friend." As the guard moved off, Gideon turned back to Stuart. "There are disturbing reports coming from outlying areas, especially near the flood zone. Groups of villagers are being rounded up and sold like cattle. The stories are spreading like wild fires around townships in the cities. People are upset. They blame the government, and so they should."

Stuart stopped walking. "What are you talking about? Slave trade?"

"Exactly. Old men and women are left behind, but the young are all taken. Especially the girls."

Stuart stopped cold. "You serious?"

"I'm afraid so."

"Who is doing this?" Stuart asked.

"That is the problem." Gideon stared at the ground. "I think it is our own people. The reports indicate these gangs are working around the entire flood zone from Zambia to Mozambique. Anywhere people are isolated, they are vulnerable. No one is watching. Few are left behind."

"I thought you said they don't take the old people. Certainly these would have some idea who is leading this nightmare."

"They do, in truth, leave the old behind; they leave them dead. Only a handful got away by running into the bush."

"This is almost too fantastic to believe," Stuart replied. "You're sure about this?"

"Yes. I am quite sure. And what is more, the abductions began before the Kariba Dam failed. Some sources say entire villages in the flood zone were disappearing just before the dam failed." Chipinduka wiped his face. "It is almost as if they knew it was going to happen. I don't know how much to believe, but I know it is not all a lie."

"What do you need from me?" Stuart asked.

"The people are losing confidence in their new government. This isn't helping. Economic growth is slow. They don't understand how long it takes to rebuild an economy that has been ravaged. Some think I am behind it, using the sale of slaves to finance this." He pointed around at the presidential grounds.

"That is nonsense." Stuart was angry.

"Yes. But people need a reason to trust me."

Stuart turned and stared out across the gardens. "What do you propose?"

"A man cannot stop the sale of any product if there is still a buyer. The drug trade is a case in point. My people have been working hard on this. We have narrowed down the destination to the Mediterranean. Soon we will have a name."

"What then?"

"I want you to create a mobile team able to deliver justice. Of course, I cannot ask the governments of Turkey, or Greece, or wherever, if I can send in a kill team. But that is what I intend to do. Where an evil man operates outside of the controls and laws of his own country, justice must also happen outside of those controls. Diplomacy does not help those who are not protected by the laws of state.

"We will determine who is enslaving these people. We will find them. And we will make it better for them to have never lived."

Chapter 33
Danbury, CT

The bikers didn't believe in strong drink while riding. Beer, however, was not strong drink and they made several stops in Danbury where the group took some time to get to know their newest charge. At each stop they made sure Zachary was surrounded by more interesting characters. Invariably, people's eyes were drawn to the tattooed heads and long braided beards. The lead biker, affectionately called Fat Man, had been a blood brother to Maurice before he got picked up on a drug dealing charge and put in the can. In spite of the spikes and tats and weird hair, the men were just regular people, though generally happier than those he encountered in the workplace.

Maurice must have been owed some significant favors, Zachary mused. The news coverage heated up such that he would never have been able to travel on his own. No one expected to see him among a traveling gang of forty motorcyclists. People made space for them. The gear they brought for him fit well and smelled like sweat and old leather. Thankfully, Zachary already knew how to ride. Maurice even sent him a wad of cash, enough to see him through to his destination in Washington, D.C.

Zachary made a mental note to stop into Maurice's restaurant when this blew over to thank him personally.

He sighed and stared into his foam cup. The coffee tasted terrible.

Fat Man wedged himself into the booth. "We aren't going to be able to pick up your girl on the bikes. Sometimes one can hide by being conspicuous. This is not one of those times." Fat Man nodded toward the counter. "Man, you've got problems. I just saw you on the news back there."

"You don't know the half of it." Zachary put down his cup.

"What's the matter?" Fat Man asked.

"You a certified counselor?" Zachary raised his eyebrows.

"Hell, yes. Hit me. What's your other problem?"

"Nothing, except my hope-to-be fiancée probably doesn't want to be in a relationship with a convict."

"Yep. I'm qualified for that."

"What do you mean?"

"Well, to start with, I *am* a convict," Fat Man said it like he was making a confession to a priest, "and I've been married a few times. Lots of experience with marriage."

"Thanks." Zach sighed. "You're a real help.

"Damn government." Fat Man made a face.

"What?" Zachary was lost.

"Government. That's your problem. If only a man could get love and get laid without the government trying to slip in between the sheets."

Zach was lost. Fat Man was probably still somewhere back in Vietnam.

"You should have brought her with you." Fat Man continued.

"Yes, well, I'm kind of new at this game."

"Give me your old phone," Fat Man held out his hand and took the phone. He turned it over and pressed the button. "How long has this been off?"

"I turned it off as soon as I went on the lam."

"Did you make or take any calls while you were with your girl?" Fat Man asked.

"Yes. One from my boss. One from the dead guy."

"Shit. We're going to have to hurry. And we've got to send this phone away. It might serve to throw them off. I've got a couple of boys who like their rides long and hard." He turned and motioned to a red-headed biker sporting a neatly cropped Fu Manchu. "Stalin, come over here."

"Stalin?" Zachary raised his eyebrows. "I don't even want to know."

Stalin moved over to the booth and leaned his knuckles on the edge of the table. The man was missing both pinkies. STALIN was tattooed across the back of the six remaining fingers. "Yes, boss."

Fat Man took Zachary's old phone and slid it across the table. "I want you to take a drive to Chicago. Turn on the phone when you leave New York State. As soon as it is on, it is going to be hot. We need to make a rabbit trail. Somewhere in Chicago, sit for a few hours then drop it in a taxi. After that, you can come back."

A smile pushed out one side of Stalin's Fu Manchu. "Playing cat and mouse, are we?"

"Exactly." As Stalin turned to go, Fat man said, "Stalin, you'll need to make good time. That phone needs to get hot sooner than later. We could use a distraction."

"My pleasure, Fat Man."

Chapter 34
New York City

Vinny sat on a park bench watching foot traffic. He pulled a phone from his pocket.

"Dead Man calling," Vinny said aloud. He dialed the new number Zachary Morgan gave him and waited. After a few rings, Zachary picked up.

"What do you want?" Morgan wasn't wasting time on pleasantries.

Vinny smiled. The plan worked brilliantly. The entire police force of New York State had Zachary's picture and the story played well on the news.

"I want original copies of Michi's investments," Vinny said.

"And what if I don't give them to you?"

"Then I make sure the fireman dies." Vinny scratched at the stubble under his chin. Just another day on the job.

"Bastard."

"Very true," he replied. "I will always be a bastard, and you will always be in jail."

Vinny could hear noise on the other end of the line while Morgan thought. Other people around him. Some kind of public place.

"Okay. Let's say I give them to you. What assurance do I have that you can turn off the heat?"

"Difficult to trust a murderer, no?" Vinny laughed. "You expect some kind of assurance from a man who can't even be counted on to feed his cat? I can tell you this: I'm a man of convictions. I can assure you the fireman will face no further complications, at least from me. And I will not kill you unless you decide to start talking. Of course, no one would believe you without evidence, and there is a good chance no one will even want to listen to you."

"So you want me to give you what I have in exchange for nothing?" Morgan sounded agitated.

"Of course. You give me what I want, and I'll do nothing."

"But if I give you what I have, I'll go to jail for murder anyway."

"Maybe. The old man was almost dead. You can probably find a lawyer to get you off on that one. Maybe downgrade it to involuntary manslaughter. This is New York after all. You'll go to jail, but not for murder."

A pause. "You're serious."

Vinny smiled. The man was starting to understand. "Mr. Morgan, you can do whatever you want. You should have evaluated the cost before you started digging around in another man's business. Just remember, if you don't give me what I want, I am forced to get more involved. I have to go looking for your loved ones, for example. And I make sure the fireman dies. You won't get *that* taken off your record. Especially not in this state. Besides, Captain Conrad Blake is a national hero."

"Why should I believe you?"

"Because you have no choice," Vinny replied.

"And what if I call the police and tell them about you?"

Vinny watched a jogger run past him. "Mr. Morgan, I already have. How did you think they fingered you so easily?" There was silence on the line. "By the way, Mr. Morgan, did I mention Captain Blake has twin boys? He left their birthday party to put out the fire you started. Such a shame."

Chapter 35
Peacock Farm, Zimbabwe

Stuart stood on the veranda of the guest cottage and looked out across his land. The main house was destroyed in the recent political upheaval, but the guest cottage escaped the flames. Kathy managed in the smaller place. They set aside plans to rebuild the main house.

Stuart had a team ready for the president. Men who preferred a direct approach—men who were persuaded that if people are not protected by society, justice has to operate outside of the law.

President Chipinduka made it clear he could not be connected. Zimbabwe was too fragile to endure international scandal. It was difficult enough to entice foreign investment back into the country.

But the President provided excellent intelligence.

Stuart sat on a camp chair and poured himself a whiskey. Soon they would know their target. Until then, they would have to wait.

Chapter 36
Pawling, New York

Zachary Morgan snapped the phone shut and stopped himself from throwing it across the parking lot. He walked over to Fat Man and Cheerio. Cheerio was one of three men without any hair at all. An English man who had gotten lost on his way home. A black ring pulled down the corner of his hairless eyebrow in a permanent squint. "You got a minute?"

"What's up?" Fat Man popped a handful of raisins into his mouth.

"I just got a call from Dead Guy." It seemed a fitting name for someone who used a dead man's phone to make his calls. "He wants the file on his boss. If he gets that, I won't have anything to prove my story. The justice system doesn't run far on 'because-I-said-so'."

"So why give it to him?"

"Because he's threatening to finish off the fireman if I don't. That would seal my fate in the legal system or effectively keep me on the lam for the rest of my life."

"That a problem?" Cheerio asked.

"Not for you, maybe. But I have a job which I kind of like. I also have a girl that I want to marry."

"So?" Fat Man spoke through a mouthful. "Living on the lam's not so bad."

Zachary tried to hold his impatience. It didn't seem profitable to argue ethics with the leader of a motorcycle gang running on the wrong side of the law since the Vietnam War. "Listen, she isn't as liberated as some of the women you hang out with. She still thinks crooks belong in jail."

"Some do." Fat Man turned the raisin box upside down and shook it, trying to get the last sticky raisin out of the corner.

Cheerio piped in, "Did you ask her?"

"Ask her what?"

"Did you ask her to marry you?"

Morgan didn't want to answer that one. "Sore subject."

"She said no?" Fat Man tried not to smile.

"No." Zachary stalled. "I chickened out."

Fat Man laughed aloud. "No shit." He raised his voice so the rest of the leather around him could hear. "You're not afraid to butt heads with the mob, but you're afraid to ask a girl to marry you. You've got it bad."

The group followed the announcement with a round of whistling, hooting and rude comments. Morgan felt like he was in middle school.

"Listen. I have maybe three minutes until Dead Man figures out that I've got a girl and goes after her. If that happens, I'm going to give them what they want, and I'm going to lose the girl, because the State of New York thinks I'm a criminal. As we've already established, my girl doesn't date criminals.

"Furthermore, I don't want that fireman to die; the guy has kids."

Fat Man tossed the raisin box. "Time to go pick her up. Call and let her know you're coming."

The three walked into a thrift store and after some tomfoolery got Fat Man fitted with something like ordinary clothing for the short hop over to Poughkeepsie. They would pick her up in a car.

For his part, Fat Man was not impressed. He looked at himself in the store mirror and scowled. "I look like a bird."

"A fat bird," Cheerio offered.

"And colorful," Zachary added, though after leather and tired jeans, any color on Fat Man looked garish.

Zachary's woolen cap had stringy hair affixed to the inside. The cap definitely looked like the gag it was, but with his half beard and torn jeans, the greasy hair was pretty believable. One of the guys added black eye liner to give a hint of Goth glory. Zachary had to admit the effect was remarkable. Even I wouldn't recognize me, he thought.

Chapter 37
New York Stock Exchange
Wall Street, New York City

Detective Stevens pulled his cruiser alongside the curb and punched a button for the four-ways. Foot traffic largely ignored him. An attractive young woman in business suit and sneakers almost bumped into him. He smiled and touched his hat. He watched her walk by before turning toward the hot dog stand.

The line dwindled. Vinny didn't waste time. People who wanted pretty food didn't buy hot dogs on the street.

"What can I get you?" Vinny asked.

"Just a chili dog." The detective reached into his pocket and pulled out a bill. He glanced behind. No one was listening. "We just got a lead. Your man had a girl."

Vinny handed over the chili dog. "You going to get her?"

The detective pulled his sunglasses from his pocket and put them on. "I'm going out now. If we don't find her there, I'll start working my way down the list of family. I'll probably have her by this evening."

Chapter 38
Lakshanya Brookes' Apartment
Old Town Alexandria, Virginia

One email message showed up in the secure box addressed to Colette Logan. Few had the address.

Colette slammed the laptop shut. Never again would she make an agreement with Ciro Michi. She didn't want to be implicated in his dirty business. The stakes were too high.

The last job, she had agreed to. Killing the Italian engineer who figured out how to destroy Kariba Dam had been a pleasure, of sorts. It felt like justice. But that had given her nightmares. All his jobs seemed to be ending that way. How long until it was her turn?

She could still hear the sound of the man screaming as the crocodile twisted off his leg, see bone protruding from skin, shaking in shock.

She wanted to take a shower and wash it all away. But she was in too deep. For the first time, Colette felt like the man owned her. She didn't want any more contract work. The senator job was different. She didn't have to work under Michi for that one. The Senator was dirt anyway. Tray's plan to use a remote camera had been brilliant. The tape of the senator groping her turned out perfectly.

Colette went to the shower. Maybe it would calm her down. Slipping out of her sweatshirt and yoga pants she stepped under hot water. Maybe this would be different. All Michi wanted this time was for her to deliver his yacht. An easy job.

"This is not a vacation," she spoke aloud. The soap slipped from her hands and skittered around the tile. Colette cornered it with her feet. She wanted to be rid of him, to forget she ever knew him. To run away from the nightmares that kept her awake.

If it hadn't been for the nightmares she might be okay. It started because she watched the news. She hadn't been ready for that amount of death. There were times in the dark when she could feel the demons crawling over her bed, their hands about her neck whispering, 'you killed them all.' Eventually she would wake up. Sometimes the demons visited while she was awake.

She toweled off and pulled on a terrycloth robe. Colette knew about traps. She created them. Extortion. Blackmail. She was a master. She pulled a wrapper and a pinch of marijuana from a zippered pouch and began to roll the joint.

Maybe she needed a priest. Needed confession.

The last time she was in confession was part of another trap. The priest seemed as eager to pay her for silence as he had been to put his hands on her.

Maybe she would try it for real. Right. She winced at the thought. Father, it has been seven years since my last confession. I helped to murder five million people. Any chance I can be forgiven?

Of course not, she thought. She would be willing to put up with hell later, if she could sleep nights without the strangulating horror of guilt. It hadn't been completely her fault. She hadn't known what she was doing—how bad it would be. She thought they were just going to damage the dam, not break it entirely. Or had she known all along? Was she blind because she wanted to be? She fought with cardboard matches and failed.

Colette cursed.

There had to be a way to get out of this. It was getting dark outside and already the night panic crept in. She wanted to be free of the monsters. Then, quite suddenly, an idea that had been formulating inconclusively in her mind stood out clearly. She knew exactly what to do.

A match finally lit and Colette drew the acrid smoke deep into her lungs, lay back on her bed and waited for the drug to take effect.

Chapter 39
Poughkeepsie, New York

The bikers didn't feel right in a car, but for now, the motorcycles were their cover and they didn't want to blow that. Fat Man grew increasingly agitated as they got closer to Poughkeepsie.

Fat Man kept his eyes on the road and both hands on the wheel of their rental car. "You sure she is going to be home?"

"I think so. If not, we can go in through the service entrance and wait for her." Zachary said.

During the drive, they talked through their plan, attempting to cover every contingency. Zach tried not to think about Serena's reaction to joining up with a mostly criminal motorcycle gang. Thankfully, her mother would be at work. That would keep it simpler.

At last they turned down the street toward the apartment complex where her mother lived. Fat man slowed and swore. "Who invited them?"

A squad car sat parked in front of her apartment building. "Down in back." Fat Man ordered. He drove by slowly, glaring at the officer.

"I love police," Cheerio said, his voice flat and humorless.

Morgan peeked through the back window.

"Where is that service entrance?" Fat Man asked.

"Around back. Look for the loading dock."

Fat Man accelerated around to the rear of the building. He pulled the Toyota up against the rubber bumper of the loading dock. "Put on your hair hat." Fat Man ordered before getting out.

They pushed their way through the door marked, 'Employees Only' and walked down a tiled hall until they found the stairway. Zachary followed Fat Man who moved remarkably fast for his size. Cheerio stayed in the downstairs hallway to keep watch.

"Right here," Zachary said. He pointed off the landing.

They stopped and Fat Man peeked in through the square glass in the door.

"Look." Fat Man whispered. A police officer was already at the door, checking the apartment number on a note pad. "I guess he's here because of you."

Zachary slumped against the wall. "Now what?"

Fat Man scowled. "What do you mean?"

"We can't go in there and bump off a policeman," Zachary protested.

"The problem with you is you still trust those guys." He shook his head sadly. "They're not here because she has overdue parking tickets."

Fat Man opened the door and stepped into the hallway. Zachary followed behind, keeping his eyes down. One very large man in a Hawaiian shirt with a greasy-haired, tag-along.

The officer glanced at them and turned back to ring the doorbell. The two slowed their pace. Someone worked the latch on the other side. As the door opened, Fat Man pulled a snub nosed pistol from his belt, pressed the cold metal against the policeman's neck and pushed him into the room.

Serena saw the men, let out a scream and bolted back into the apartment. Zachary slipped behind Fat Man and shut the door. Fat Man slammed the officer into the wall, relieved him of his weapon, and shoved him into a powder room. There Fat Man lifted the seat and made the man kneel over the commode where Zachary fastened the officer's hands together underneath the tank with his own cuffs.

Fat Man laughed aloud. "Perfect," he said before they turned to leave the powder room.

Serena was waiting for them. A wall of mace smashed into Fat Man who doubled over in time for Zachary to get a face full. It clawed its way up their sinuses, pounded inside their heads, and burnt its way down their throats. Serena bolted out the door and down the hall.

Fat Man and Zachary fled the cloud of spray in the bathroom and groped their way to the kitchen sink where they fought each other for water. The officer grunted and tried to stifle the over-spray by stuffing his head as far as possible down inside the toilet. Residual spray hung in the tiny room and wormed its way into his pores.

#

Serena raced toward the emergency stairs. The elevator was too slow. She crashed hard into the door before seeing the 'Pull' sign. Hot air from the stairs seemed to crowd around her. The echo of her own footsteps sounded like someone following. No time to think. She needed to find the police. Had to get away. First a police officer showed up unannounced, then a couple of thugs tried to take him out. It didn't make sense. Where in the hell was Zachary? She groped her pocket for the cell phone she had left in the apartment. It was her only link to Zachary, but she couldn't go back now.

Serena jumped the last few steps and exited into the lobby of her apartment building. A custodian wheeled a yellow bucket and mop out of a nearby janitor's closet.

"Help!" Serena called. "Call the police."

The custodian shrugged and pointed toward the front doors. "There's a cop out there."

She sprinted across the lobby and out the front doors. A plain-clothes police officer stood leaning against the squad car.

"Help me. I'm being chased." Serena almost ran into the man.

The man jumped to attention and opened the back door of the cruiser. "Quick. Get in."

He shut the door behind her and ran around to the driver's seat. Then he punched on the emergency lights and peeled away from the curb, leaving a group of startled pedestrians standing in a cloud of burning rubber and exhaust.

#

Water had done practically nothing to stop the effect of the spray. Zachary rummaged for milk and poured it into Fat Man's eyes. It ran over his face and dripped off the edges of his beard. The relief was almost immediate. They removed their hat-wigs wiped their faces and necks on a dishtowel. Zachary pulled out his phone and fought with teary eyes to dial Serena's number. Her phone buzzed on the buffet table.

"Damn it." Zachary hung up.

"I've heard of playing hard to get, but your girl treats it like an extreme sport." Fat Man hocked and spat again into the sink. "I can't get rid of that awful taste."

"Hurry up. We've got to get her," Zachary said.

Fat Man squared up to Zachary and held him by the shoulders. "Dude. She's gone."

"Then I've got to get those documents from my safe deposit box. Now that the police are on to Serena, Dead Guy is going to connect the dots. It's only a matter of time until he catches up with her and gives me another call." And this time, he would have more leverage.

"I don't do bank jobs." Fat Man's eyes were swollen. He walked to the mirror over the fireplace mantle. He poked at the red, puffy bags under his eyes. "I look like a bad hangover."

"No one is going to care what you look like. The problem is me. I'm the one people are looking for."

"Where is the bank?" Fat Man asked.

Zachary motioned with his chin toward the bathroom where the police officer was still kneeling.

"Right." Fat Man winked and lowered his voice. "Let's not disturb the good reverend at his prayers."

The two headed for the door. Zachary peered through the peephole, then cracked the door enough to check the hallway.

"Let's go." Zachary jogged back toward the stairwell. His throat was still on fire, but they didn't have time to stop and lick their wounds.

Zach glanced at his red-faced friend. "You look fat."

"No shit. I'm swollen all the way down to my ass." Fat Man replied. "Where is this bank?"

"Do you like old people?" Zachary led the way down the stairs.

"No. I don't like old people, and I don't like riddles."

"Perfect." Zachary pushed open the door into the downstairs lobby. "Where's Cheerio?"

The two emerged from the stairwell, conscious of their tearing eyes and red faces. They retraced their steps to the service door. It was only a matter of time before the cop woke up and started shouting.

Fat Man grumbled. "Crazy Brit. He's always disappearing at the worst times."

"What do you mean?" They reached the rental. Cheerio was nowhere to be seen.

"How do you think he got his name? Let's get moving." Fat Man climbed in behind the wheel and fought to get the key in the ignition.

"We're just going to leave without him?"

"Yeah. He'll show up sometime. Always does. Sometimes it's with a new bike. Sometimes with a new chick. But he'll come back. We don't know where he goes or how he finds us, so we've just stopped asking questions." Fat Man pulled away and entered traffic, his shoulders tense.

"So what's the problem with banks?"

"Too many cameras. I'm wanted in nine states, and there are too many cameras in a bank for me."

"Forty-nine?" Zachary raised his eyebrows.

Fat Man shrugged. "Can't ride to Hawaii. I don't do planes."

Zachary shook his head. "Okay, note to self: scary biker dude is afraid of planes, cameras and old people."

"Where are we going anyway?" Fat Man looked grumbled.

"To visit grandma."

Chapter 40
East Potomac Park, Washington, D.C.

The secretary for Zimbabwe's Mission to the United States followed a consistent routine. Colette sat on a park bench in East Potomac Park. She didn't have to wait long. The secretary jogged toward her on the path.

Overhead, a UPS freight plane banked for its final descent to Washington's Dulles International Airport.

Zimbabwe's ambassador happened to be home attending a funeral, but the consular offices continued to keep regular hours. Colette wasn't interested in regular hours. She had no desire to get arrested. She just needed to get rid of Ciro Michi and her nightmares. Hopefully taking care of the first would solve the second.

It surprised Colette that the woman was a runner. Spandex and African women didn't seem to be a particularly ethnic combination. The embassy woman was probably in her early thirties, but looked younger. Perspiration made her black skin shine. Time to go.

She turned and started running, adjusting her pace so the woman would catch up. Colette settled into a comfortable rhythm, listening always to the sounds of feet behind her. A bicycle passed on her left, and then she heard the secretary coming.

"Hello, Maureen." Colette startled her.

The woman turned. A smile. "Do I know you?" Typical African friendliness.

"No, you don't, but I would like to speak with you, if I may."

They stopped running. "How do you know my name?" Maureen asked.

Colette returned the smile. No threats. "I'm afraid I can't tell you, but I would like to help your country."

A shadow crossed Maureen's face. "What do you know of my country?"

"I know the destruction of the Kariba Dam was not an accident." Colette decided the direct approach would be most effective. Their interaction needed to be brief.

Maureen's eyebrows went up. This was not just a friendly encounter.

Colette spoke softly. "I am going to send you a detailed fax over your secure embassy line. It will arrive on your desk at exactly 8:30 tomorrow morning. This fax will outline how the dam was weakened so it would break when the spillway gates were opened to relieve seasonal flooding. It will name the person ultimately responsible for the disaster.

"You may pass along my contact information to the presidents of Zambia and Zimbabwe as you see fit. Colette handed her a card with an email address, but no name. "Do not give this contact information to anyone else, or I will no longer be able to help you."

"And how do I know you are telling me the truth about all this?" the secretary asked.

Colette Logan stared at the Potomac before looking back into Maureen's eyes. "Because I helped to do it."

Chapter 41
New York

Soon after leaving the apartment complex, the officer turned off the emergency lights. Outside of Poughkeepsie, he pulled the cruiser into a truck stop and parked between several rigs, hiding from view.

Serena felt an odd prickle of fear. It didn't add up. She grew more and more certain something wasn't right.

The officer turned off the vehicle and knocked on the glass to get her attention. "I've got to use the loo. You want some coffee?" His accent was decidedly British.

"Sure. Where are you—?"

"I'll be right back." He slammed the door and walked to the concession area. A couple of long-haul truckers milled around outside, likely sharing news on routes, weigh-stations and hookers.

Serena watched the officer stop and talk to them. One of the truckers, a thin, muscular man in faded jeans and cowboy boots glanced in her direction. Serena tried the latch on the door. Locked.

The officer finished his conversation and went inside, she assumed, to relieve himself. The other men dispersed when he left and walked back to their trucks. The young man looked in her direction once again before climbing in his rig.

A few minutes later, the officer reappeared and walked toward the cruiser with two cups of coffee.

He set the cups on the roof and opened her door.

"We're going to have to move. The boys agreed to help. There's a loading ramp around back."

"Why aren't we going to the police station?" Serena asked.

He crouched in front of her. "You're kidding, right?"

She didn't respond.

"You don't really think I'm a police officer do you?" The man seemed genuinely surprised. She saw a rod piercing his eyebrow. Odd uniform for a cop.

"Actually, I did."

"You are a bit slow then, aren't you luv?" He shook his head and muttered. "I thought that—well never mind. We're tangling with some bad men, and if we hang around here long enough, they're bound to catch up with us."

Serena felt like bolting past the man and screaming for help, but he was crouched in front of her door, and he didn't act like she were his prisoner.

"I'd love to explain, but we are in a bit of a hurry. Do you mind if we get moving? I'll explain later."

He handed her a cup. "One cream, one sugar, right?"

"Yes. How did you know that?" she asked.

"Mr. Morgan."

The words stunned her.

"Zachary?" she whispered.

"That's the one." He glanced around them. "Can we go now?"

"Who are you?" Serena asked.

"Cheerio's the name. Friend of a friend of a friend. I think." He counted this out on his fingers then shook his head. "Doesn't matter really. We need to move. The cruiser is going one way. We're going another."

She nodded dumbly. "Where to?"

Chapter 42
Hope Retirement Community
Brewster, New York.

Zachary Morgan and Fat Man walked into the main lobby of Hope Retirement Community. The foyer boasted a fabulous glass ceiling supported by grand marble columns. A central fountain cascaded over a rocky bed of moss and fern.

"Jeez. Some place." Fat Man stared up at the sun through glass.

"Right. I guess this is supposed to soften the blow of getting old." Zachary nodded toward the far corner. "Bank's over there." Nation's First sat nestled between a nail salon and an indoor café complete with patio furniture looking out onto the fountain area.

"You put the papers there?" Fat Man asked.

"Yep. Right after I retrieved them from Travis Sander's safe. Granny, Aunt Sadie, actually, is my god-mother. No blood ties to follow. I figured it would be as secure as any. Cameras are one thing, but this place has a bunch of old people with nothing better to do than knit and gossip."

They approached a reception area off to one side where Zachary signed a visitors' book with a fake name. He led the way past the fountain area to a hall that extended away from the lobby. They had a limited amount of time before Dead Guy found out about Serena. Zachary tried to concentrate on the next thing he had to do to find her and keep her safe. Get the documents. Wait for the call. Make the drop.

"Here it is." Zachary stopped in front of Apartment D4 and knocked.

After a few moments, the door opened. The woman before them stood only as tall as Zachary's shoulder. She was all wrinkles and grey, but her eyes were sharp and blue.

"Well, well. Look who has finally come to visit Aunt Sadie." She took his face in both hands and gave him a kiss on his lips. "And about time, I was needing some company."

Zachary introduced Fat Man. "Granny, this is Charles Hoake. He's a friend of mine."

"Come in, come in." She turned and led them to the kitchen. "You boys are probably hungry." Sadie settled them at the table. The apartment afforded semi-independent living for those who could still function on their own.

"Actually, Granny, we can't stay long. We're on a business trip of sorts. I figured we had just enough time to stop in for a quick visit." He didn't want to tell her too much.

"Nonsense. You have to eat anyway. Might as well be here—" She fussed in the refrigerator, ignoring Zachary's protests.

Zachary rolled his eyes at Fat Man. "Granny—"

"I'll whip up some toasted cheese sandwiches. You'll have to get the pickle jar open for me, Charlie; I don't have the strength in my hands anymore. I'm so glad you've come."

"Granny, really. I'm not sure we have the time."

"Don't talk back to me, Zachary," she said sternly. "Tell him, Charlie."

Fat Man's face soured at the sound of his real name, and he shrugged awkwardly.

Aunt Sadie grabbed a loaf of bread and brought it to the table. "Charlie. I want you to butter six pieces on both sides. Nice and even now. "Zachary, get the sliced cheddar out of the deli drawer."

Zachary started to speak then reconsidered.

Fat Man labored over the bread and butter like an art student working out his final brush strokes. Aunt Sadie placed the sandwiches on a hot griddle.

"So what brings you boys out this way?" Aunt Sadie talked as she tended their food.

"I told you, Granny, we're on business."

Aunt Sadie eyed him suspiciously. "That so?"

Zachary looked at Fat Man for help. Nothing.

Aunt Sadie put paper towels around her kitchen table to serve as plates.

She poured water and sat them down. "Charlie, you say grace."

He looked terrified. Aunt Sadie closed her eyes and folded her hands like a girl in Sunday school.

Fat Man muttered under his breath. The 'amen' was clear.

The boys ate in silence while Aunt Sadie nattered away about the other residents. She talked as if the boys already knew them and kept abreast of all the current health and family issues.

Finally, Zachary couldn't wait any longer. He knew they would have to get to the in-house bank before it closed or he might not get another chance. As of yet, he hadn't received a call from Dead Guy. No call meant Dead Guy hadn't found out about Serena. It was only a matter of time. "Granny, I need to get to the bank and get the file that I left here."

"Nonsense. You haven't finished your sandwich. Charlie can walk me down, and we can get the file. Besides," she rummaged through her bureau drawer for identification, "you had better not go in there. With your face all over the news, someone is liable to

105

recognize you." She took Charlie by the arm and led him out the door.

Chapter 43
Zimbabwean Embassy
Washington, D.C.

Maureen Kampala sat at her desk, sipping coffee.

She slept badly after yesterday's interaction in the park. In the darkness of night, Maureen decided the woman was crazy. But by morning, she wasn't so sure. As of yet, she hadn't determined what, if anything, to report about the conversation. What was there to say?

That a woman stopped her and said that the largest disaster on record in Southern Africa was partially her fault? It didn't matter that the woman seemed rational. It didn't matter that the woman seemed sincere, sorry even. The story ran short on facts.

She glanced at the fax machine. Maureen opened her secure email to begin reading the morning briefing.

At precisely 8:30 the fax machine came to life.

Maureen set down her coffee and held her breath as the fax came in. She looked at the caller identification number and immediately ran a search on her computer. Office supply store. Public fax. Maureen started reading before they had finished printing. She pushed aside the other files on the glass-topped desk. Then she spread out all three pages in order and looked at them. Typed. Times New Roman. 12 point font. Single spaced. First person. No signature. No name. Headings in bold. Bulleted points. European spellings.

The narrative was clear and articulate. Obviously this hadn't been written in a hurry. It outlined the operation from start to finish. It was immediately apparent the author had been to Kariba Lake. It included an itemized list of materials and supplies needed for an operation apparently carried out from a house boat rented on the Zimbabwe side. The memo identified the specific demolition agent as Dexpan, a non-explosive charge to weaken the dam between spillway gates.

Maureen noticed a change in tone when the author explained the technicalities of the underwater part. One simple sentence, set off from the others, stood out:

I allowed myself to believe the purpose of the operation was merely to damage the dam.

Included was the woman's compensation in US dollars. The report indicated a second operative, but carefully left out any kind of distinguishing information. Male, female, height, race, country of origin. She only said he was not from Zimbabwe or Zambia. For some reason the author found that important.

Funding for the job had come from a prominent Italian. Though details were sparing, Maureen felt the author wanted to divulge more, but net yet. The next step in the dance.

The last page was a copy of the contact. Though the resolution was poor, its import was clear. A contract for the reconstruction of the dam had been authorized by none other than the Honorable Cedric Banda Mwanyisa, the recently deposed dictator of Zimbabwe.

Maureen's hands felt cold.   Until now, she had held out the possibility that the letter was just a hoax. Not any more. Evil ran deeper than color. She knew that already. It wasn't as simple as hating the colonial bastards who foisted their imperial system and avarice on the people of Central Africa.

She didn't know what to make of the woman's roundabout offer to help. The damage had already been done. She thought about it for a moment.

Zimbabwe's dictator was dead. Maureen wondered if Mwanyisa's assassins knew about the plot against the Kariba Dam and hoped killing Mwanyisa would stop it. She would probably never know. But the Italian was still very much alive.

If the Kariba disaster really was an act of terrorism, the only work left to do was administer justice.

Chapter 44
Portland, Maine

DeShawn Ford pulled his rig off the highway via the Portland exit. He would unload here and complete his run up to Bar Harbor area where he was scheduled to pick up a load of granite for counter tops. Counter tops for people who made more money than he did. He wouldn't trade his life. DeShawn liked trucking, owning his own rig and being his own boss.

DeShawn worked his way through traffic toward a lumber yard. He turned into the empty parking lot a few minutes before closing time. Hopefully, he wasn't too late.

He jumped down from his idling rig. An electronic ding sounded as he pushed through the front door.

"We're closing in five minutes." The woman behind the counter didn't look up.

"Is that so?" DeShawn walked past the fasteners and caulk tubes before peeking around the end of rack.

"Hi, Lena."

"Oh, it's you. What are you doing here? I thought you didn't work this route anymore."

"My load's shifted. I need to get her squared again before I get back on the road." He stopped and shoved his hands in his pockets. "It's my mama's birthday tomorrow, and I promised I'd be home in time. But this load is giving me hell. Any chance I could use the forklift for five minutes?"

She pointed through the back doors. "Out there on your left. Keys are under the seat."

"Fantastic."

"The yard man's gone already. He knocks off at 4:30. Just be sure to put it back where you found it."

The old yellow fork lift was parked under an overhang next to a shack where the boys would take customer pick-up slips. He started it up and pulled it around front to his truck.

DeShawn maneuvered the loader next to the trailer and lifted the police cruiser off the flat bed. It was still covered in a green tarpaulin. He backed up and carefully set it down in a parking spot next to the main entrance of the hardware store.

Then he returned the fork lift to its spot. Lena was waiting for him with her hands on her hips.

"Was that a car you unloaded?" She scowled at him.

"Yes, ma'am."

"I thought you were just going to shift your load."

"Yes, ma'am. I shifted the load from there to there." DeShawn pointed from the flat bed to the parking lot and smiled.

"Are you going to get me in trouble?"

"Now, don't you worry," DeShawn said, "The way I see it, you were closed and gone before this all happened. Besides, this ain't nothing more than a practical joke.

He climbed back into his rig and gave her a wave. She ignored him, turned back into the store, and flipped the 'Open' sign to 'Closed'

Chapter 45
New York, New York

The record store boasted an impressive selection of vintage vinyl and turntables. A poorly painted rainbow decorated the shop window, and a fairy creature painted below called in customers who needed a fresh bag of marijuana. The real money-making business.

Cheap Christmas bells attached to the door failed to rouse a half-stoned, thin woman behind the register. Detective Stevens knocked on the counter, and she turned around, eyes black and empty.

"I'm looking for Vinny," he said.

"I love your shirt, man. That the real thing?" She drawled and reached across the counter to touch his uniform.

"Yes, and I'm in a hurry."

She looked him over. "Too bad." She took a long, slow pull on a joint and blew the smoke toward him. "Vinny ain't around."

"Where can I find him?"

"Do I look like his mother?" Her sneer pushed up the ring in her lip.

Stevens reached across the counter to grab a fist-full of shirt and yanked her toward him. Nose to nose. He was not in the mood.

"Would you like to help me or would you like me to haul your skinny ass in for dealing?" His breath was hot and close. "What is your name?"

"Ava," she stammered out the answer.

"Ava, I'm about to get impatient. I need to find Vinny, and you are going to help me."

"Geez. Chill out." She tried to push herself back. The counter edge dug into her, but the officer tightened his grip and pulled harder.

"I'll chill out when you tell me where he is."

"Okay, man, he's upstairs." She pointed to a staircase beyond the stacked boxes of record sleeves with men in bellbottoms and long pointed collars.

Detective Stevens gave the woman a shove and headed for the stairs.

Vinny sat on a tired-out couch reading a decades-old National Geographic magazine. "You find the girl?" Vinny asked.

"We need to talk."

Vinny lifted his hands. "What the hell are you talking about? I thought you had this wrapped up?"

"Me too, Vinny, but the girl got away. Some thugs attacked me when I got to her room. Long story. But she got away from them, too. Don't know who they were. Does Lanzo have someone else working on this broad?"

Vinny tried to digest this. "I don't know. He's getting a lot of pressure from some big shot in the old country that could make life unpleasant for us."

"When did you lose her?"

"Just a few hours ago. You're a hard guy to find."

"We may still have a chance. You doing anything tomorrow?"

"As a matter of fact, I am. I have to go into work and explain to my boss how I happened to lose a police cruiser outside of jurisdiction when I wasn't even supposed to be on duty. You're on your own."

Chapter 46
Hope Retirement Community
Brewster, New York

After they returned from the in-house bank, Aunt Sadie insisted Charlie take her for a walk to see Oscar, the resident therapy dog. Zachary alternately paced the apartment and grabbed thick handfuls of curly hair.

A beep from his cell phone jarred him back to the present. Dead Guy calling.

"This is Zachary." He snapped the phone to his ear. Afraid of what he might miss, afraid what he might find out.

"Mr. Morgan. We sent the police to pick up a lady friend of yours."

Zachary felt his head spinning. He looked for a chair. "What do you mean, we? Are you with the police department?"

"My, Mr. Morgan, you are curious. Spending too much time at the paper digging into other people's business?"

"Where is she?" Morgan demanded.

"Once again, Mr. Morgan, you are missing the point. The real question is where is the file? Already it has taken you too long. The people I work for don't like to be kept waiting. They always get what they want. Always. She is quite beautiful, you know." Dead Guy seemed to be enjoying the cat and mouse. "Perhaps we shouldn't hurry this along."

Zachary held onto the phone with both hands and forced himself to say nothing.

"Lucky for you, my boss is in a terrible rush. Or should I say, lucky for Serena."

"If you lay one finger on her, I will—"

"You will what, Mr. Morgan? You don't even know who I am."

Zachary silently cursed himself for speaking. He stood and walked the phone around Aunt Sadie's tiny apartment. "I'll meet you in D.C."

"I'm sorry; you don't get to make the rules." Dead Guy replied.

"How badly do you want the file?" Zachary tried to sound convincing. There was a pause. Dead Guy must be more desperate than he let on.

Zachary pushed forward. "The World War II memorial, Washington Mall. Noon tomorrow. I'll be standing near the section honoring Pennsylvania. If I don't see the girl, you get nothing. If I get the girl, you get your file."

Zachary hung up.

Chapter 47
Washington, D.C.

Fat Man Charlie came back to himself. Leather had a way of soothing him from the horrors of flowery shirts and old women who called him 'dear.'

He leaned against the concrete trash can in the parking lot of Denny's just outside D.C. Zachary and Fat Man caught up with the rest of the motorcycle gang and stood surrounded by bizarre paint schemes and polished chrome. The rest of the men talked or sipped coffee from Styrofoam cups.

Zachary studied the group. His leather and unshaved face made him look like one of the guys. Hiding in a crowd of loud motorcycles.

"How do we know this guy will show?" Fat Man interrupted his thoughts.

"Because I've got something he wants." Zachary tried to sound convincing.

"I don't see what is so exciting about someone with a sudden interest in copper shares."

"Long story. I'm going to leave the real paper copy with you until I have Serena in hand. If there is any funny business, I'll use it as leverage."

"There's a plan." Fat Man shook his head. "Pity we don't know what the man looks like. I don't like trading for women. Doesn't seem right. He has the girl—all you've got is a bunch of paper. This does not give me a good feeling." Fat Man chewed the end of a toothpick into a paintbrush. "What if he has a bunch of other thugs working with him?"

"I think with the story they're hiding, the bad guys are going to want to keep the circle small."

"You really are a trusting kind of guy. What if he has a sniper?"

"In the Washington Mall? Unlikely."

Fat Man shook his head and got on his bike. "Whatever you say. It's your girl. Let's go get her."

Fat Man punched the starter button and split the silence of morning with thunder. One by one, down the line, the bikes started. It was their way. Faces appeared at windows, hands over ears. Some laughing; some heads shaking.

Following Fat Man and Zach, the group of bikes exited the restaurant parking lot in synchronized twos. Traffic stopped to let them out with the deference given a funeral procession.

Chapter 48

Serena and Cheerio hitched a ride on the sleeper truck of a friend Cheerio made at the rest stop. She marveled at how easily Cheerio convinced people to help him. Maybe it was the accent.

They made small talk with the trucker until disembarking near a derelict bicycle shop in New Jersey. As the trucker moved off, Serena turned to Cheerio. "Can I make my one phone call now?"

Cheerio looked shocked. "You want to get us killed, don't you?"

"What are you talking about? I'm just going to call Zachary. He has a safe phone."

"No such thing." Cheerio sounded like a grade school teacher educating a student on the horrors of the real world. "Put one of those in your pocket and you might as well put out a flag saying, 'Here I am, come and get me'."

Serena stared at him, trying to decide if he actually believed what he was saying. "You really think the police have the new number?"

"Not just yours, luv. All of them. Every last one. The government has a master cell record collection facility under the White House." He moved in closer and whispered, "They're listening to every single phone call, even those little twelve-year-old girls who think they are secretly calling their boyfriends."

"Okay." Serena pursed her lips. He was clearly paranoid. Cheerio at least had himself convinced.

"Well then, you've got some explaining to do. I'm in serious need of answers here."

"Right-o. The officer who came to pick you up was probably working with the New York mafia. His squad car was a long way from home." As he talked, he led her around to a rusting, metal warehouse in the rear with a single wooden garage door. "I'm not exactly sure what happened in your apartment. Fat Man and Mr. Morgan were supposed to pick you up and head out the back entrance. Instead, you came flying out the front door and practically jumped into my arms." Cheerio winked. "Happens all the time."

"Zachary was there?" Serena was shocked. "I thought you were a real police officer."

"It's a good thing I wasn't. If you had been picked up by the police, it would have all been over for you and Mr. Morgan. The man who's been calling Zachary has been getting pretty ugly by the sounds of things. Even threatening to kill that fireman."

Serena put her hand on Cheerio's arm. "What fireman?"

"The same one who got hurt when he tried to save the old man at Morgan's apartment. Apparently, the mob was in a hurry to get their hands on Mr. Morgan, so they decided to make him go public."

"What do you mean, go public?" Serena was struggling to keep up.

"You know, call him an arsonist, make him a public figure of ill-repute. Works rather well, actually." Cheerio pulled a key from his pocket and worked it into a padlock hanging off the side of the garage door. "Everyone wants to find him and no one will believe anything he says. Instead of the mob doing the work, they let the police take over. When the man is found and processed, it gets much easier for them to take him out. Same thing happened to Fat Man. Media got involved. Something about the Vietnam War. Don't remember exactly."

"Who's Fat Man?"

"The leader of our biker brothers. Real name is Charlie Hoake.

They didn't get him, but he lost his family. They bought into all the nonsense they saw on the boob tube." The door squeaked as he pulled it open. He snapped on a light to illuminate the interior. No less than seven motorcycles, tightly packed in neat rows, shone with chrome and polished paint. Cheerio stared and smiled. "Now there's a thing of beauty."

"Whose are these?" Serena stepped out of the sunshine into the shed to get a closer look.

Cheerio spread his arm wide in introduction. "This is my family. They are also the fastest and least conspicuous way to get from point A to your Mr. Morgan. Which do you want to take?"

Serena felt a tingle of excitement in the prospect of seeing Zachary.

"What do you *do* for a living?" Serena asked.

Cheerio looked surprised. "I ride."

Chapter 49
New York Hospital

Lisa Blake slept uncomfortably in the guest chair beside her husband's bed in the critical care unit. The interior hall wall was made of glass. A transparent reminder that Conrad Blake required constant monitoring.

Flowers and cards surrounded Captain Conrad Blake. Crayon drawings from the first grade class at St. Anthony's covered the bulletin board. People still remembered his heroism on 9/11.
A cardiac monitor suddenly flat lined. The sound brought Lisa to her feet before she was fully awake.

"Excuse me, ma'am." A critical care nurse pushed past Lisa to her husband's side and pressed the emergency button above his headboard. Within seconds, four nurses appeared.

"Ma'am, we're going to need you to step out of the room." A nurse took her by the arm and directed her to the hall as another started chest compressions—counting out loud.

"Grant. Get the AED. I'll prep." The charge nurse ignored Lisa altogether.

Lisa moved to the other side of the glass wall and watched with horror as one nurse traded off on chest compressions. She, too, counted aloud. Another nurse unsnapped the wires for the cardiac monitor and ripped off the stickers that clung to Conrad's shaved chest. The cardiac alarm continued to sound its relentless beep in the corner.

Grant returned and set the AED near the patient's side. He opened the box and worked with another nurse to attach the patches on the patient's chest. He turned on the box and the Automatic External Defibrillator computerized voice commanded, "Please stand clear of the patient."

The fireman's chest twitched involuntarily. The nurses glanced at the cardiac monitor.

Nothing.

The AED repeated the stand clear command.

Nothing.

The charge nurse filled a syringe and nodded toward Grant. Grant turned off the machine and peeled back a patch covering the dying man's heart. Lisa stared dumbly as the nurse slid her fingers down, counting ribs, before driving the needle deep into her husband's chest. She watched with horror as the nurse depressed the plunger, squirting medicine directly into his stopped heart.

Chapter 50
Washington, D.C.
World War II Memorial
12:14 p.m.

Hot humid air pressed down on the mass of tourists walking the National Mall. Groups of Koreans pausing for pictures of each other at every turn mixed with troops of boy scouts, veteran tour guides and Washington's own businessmen and women in black and white. Several obese mothers sat fanning and sweating on park benches here and there while children, high on candy and sugar drinks, swarmed about like flies. Lovers strolled and kissed.

Everywhere people walked or milled or sat. But nowhere did Zachary see any sign of Serena. A vague panic started to press in on his mind. He didn't like to be kept waiting, and he didn't like not knowing what Dead Guy looked like.

He reached under his motorcycle vest and withdrew a manila envelope. In desperation, he held it up and waved it over his head. Maybe Dead Guy was having a hard time recognizing him as well.

"You looking for a courier?" The voice came from a short balding man beside him.

"Not exactly." Zachary turned and studied the man leaning against the monument eating a hot dog.

"Pity. Because I'm in the business." The man shoved in the last bite and licked his fingers.

"What are you talking about?" Zachary asked.

"Your girl is in the van." He motioned toward Constitution Avenue. Zachary saw a black Dodge Sprinter parked near the intersection of 17th Street.

"You were supposed to bring her with you." The voice belonged to Dead Guy, Zachary thought.

The man reached into his pocket, pulled out a white handkerchief and poked at a spot of mustard on his shirt. "Now, Mr. Morgan, surely you didn't expect me to bring her to you with no assurance that you would actually have what I want?"

"I don't believe this." Zachary shook his head.

"You have the files?" he asked, unperturbed by Zachary's frustration.

"Of course I have the files."

"Let me see them."

"First you show me Serena."

The man shrugged and replied, "Have it your way." He stuffed the handkerchief into his pocket and headed for the sidewalk on 17th.

Zachary fell in behind, mind racing with the possibility of seeing Serena again and the gnawing fear that he was playing chess with the devil. The man was broad in the shoulders, but not especially trim. Zachary might be able to outrun him if it came to that, but he didn't know if Dead Guy had other players in the field. He knew the man was capable of murder. It didn't seem fair that a man with that many scars on his conscience could amble along the sidewalk as if he hadn't a care in the world.

Dead Guy reached Constitution Avenue and turned right, keeping to the sidewalk. As they neared the van, Zachary's mind began to run scenarios. None of his musings ended well so he tried to shut it off and chalk it up to morbid fancy.

"Here we go." Dead Guy pulled a set of keys out of his pocket and unlocked the side door of the panel van. He turned back to

Zachary. "No monkey business. I let you see the girl, you give me the file, I check the file and undo the girl's cuffs so she can leave."

Zachary nodded and opened the door. The van was empty. Suddenly the man gave him a forceful shove, crushing his shins against metal and sending Zachary sprawling onto the van floor. The door slammed shut behind him.

After a few seconds, the driver's door opened and the man climbed in. A metal cargo fence behind the driver's seat effectively kept Zachary from attacking his captor.

"This isn't the file you want," Zachary tried.

"That's ok. We don't really need the file if we have you. The fire was just to keep you discredited and silent until we had a chance to pick you up."

"Where are you taking me?" Zachary demanded.

Dead Guy inserted his keys into the ignition. "We're going on a road trip."

Chapter 51
Constitution Ave.
Washington, D.C.

Spread around the World War II memorial, Fat Man's gang looked remarkably inconspicuous. They saw Zachary make contact and head toward a black Dodge Sprinter. As a group, they made a beeline for their motorcycles parked along Constitution on the west side of 17ᵗʰ Street. The entire group decorated their bikes with black Prisoner of War flags attached to antennae, handlebars or pinned onto shirts. The men waited for Fat Man to mount before they fired up.

"Boys, it's protest time." Fat Man punched the start button and thunder rolled from his bike to the others behind until all forty had come alive. Traffic stopped as they pulled out en masse.

The black van entered traffic heading east on Constitution Avenue. Fat Man closed the gap and pulled around the van as it passed 15ᵗʰ Street. A third of the riders followed Fat Man, pushing their way in front of the van, riding in tight formation, the rest stayed behind or beside, making sure the van had no way out.

Once in position, Fat Man raised his fist and the entire procession began to slow, forcing the van to stop in front of the Department of Justice.

They dismounted but left bikes running. The group coalesced around the van, waving flags and shouting, "we will never forget".

Chen T'ao, the only gang member of Chinese descent, walked to the driver's side window and shattered the glass with an armor-plated elbow. His right arm followed with a punch that dislocated the driver's jaw and sent him sprawling over the wheel. Chen followed up with a second hit and watched the man's eyes roll back.

Chen unlocked the van and a biker on the other side opened the rear door. Zachary climbed into the front passenger side of the van. Another biker tied a black and white flag to the antenna and plastered the sides with POW stickers. Zachary pulled the unconscious man from the driver's seat, moved in behind the wheel and put the van into drive. The entire exchange lasted less than twenty seconds. The bikers mounted up again and started moving with what appeared to be a matching black van, taking their protest elsewhere.

Chapter 52
Hope Retirement Community
New York

Aunt Sadie sat in front of the lounge television next to another resident. She talked to him for a while before she realized he nodded off.

"Oh, well." She sighed and got up to get the remote control Velcroed to the coffee table. The retirement home wasn't exactly the best place to pick up a date.

Sadie turned to CNN and watched stories about flooding in the Philippines and an attempted coup in some West African country. When she saw Zachary's picture on the screen behind the newscaster she sat up straight and put her crochet down. The newscaster, wrapped in a tight, short dress, changed her tone to match the story.

"A hero of the 9/11 attacks on New York City died today. Captain Conrad Blake is survived by a wife and twin boys. The governor will be in attendance at the funeral on Thursday. He has called for renewed efforts to find the suspected arsonist, Zachary Morgan, and bring him to justice.

"The search for the New York Times reporter who fled the scene has yielded nothing. Investigators close to the case suggest Morgan might also be connected to the disappearance of a freelance photographer, Serena Chavez."

Chapter 53
Zimbabwean Embassy
Washington D.C.

The parade of bikes progressed down Constitution Avenue. The thunder of exhaust drew attention from bystanders. Smiles from some, scowls from others. Zachary Morgan drove without noticing, unable to grasp that Serena was still missing. His best lead to find Serena lay unresponsive on the seat beside him.

The man killed Travis Sander, and right now Morgan wanted him alive.

Zachary drove automatically, how would he find Serena now? He still carried the ring in his pocket. A charm. A tangible talisman of hope.

What a joke, he chastised himself. Since being framed for murder he joined a gang of leatherheads, most of whom were wanted by the law. He should either turn himself in and trust the legal system or forget any hope of going back to normal life and live on the run with a motorcycle between his legs.

Fat Man dropped back to ride beside him, smiled and saluted. Zachary waved through the broken window and wondered what he was up to. The only time Zachary had seen Fat Man stressed out was while driving a car.

Fat Man worked his way past Zachary and took his place at the front of the line of bikes. He turned onto Route One and drove away from the National Mall. The rest of the bikes followed. Their sound echoed off the sides of buildings. Traffic stopped for them at intersections because they weren't given a choice. If a light turned red, the line of bikers continued through.

Most people treated it as a parade. Special privileges. Different rules. Besides, no one wanted to mess with the riders. Better to smile and get over it.

Fat Man led the motorcycle train up to Massachusetts Ave and left toward DuPont Circle. Only when they reached the circle and turned onto New Hampshire Avenue did Zachary realize where they were going. Zimbabwean Embassy. It had been part of the original plan: Get the girl, give the file to the Africans, go into hiding until... That's where it got fuzzy.

The motorcycles came to a stop in front of the unassuming Zimbabwean Embassy. A single security camera stared down at a white door. The Zimbabwean flag hung limp from its pole in front of the three story red brick building that once served as home for the Institute of Soviet-American relations. Zimbabwe's last president purchased the building in 1990.

A simple wrought-iron gate surrounded the tiny patch of grass out front. Matching iron hand rails led up concrete steps to the front door.

The parade of bikes stood idling in their lane as Zachary stepped out of the van and ascended the stairs, envelope in hand. He pressed the intercom button and stared into the camera. At times like this he wished he could have a shower and something more than jeans and leather to wear. Who would take him seriously with an entrance like this?

#

A black woman opened the door and looked out into the street before making eye contact with him.

"Mr. Zachary Morgan?"

Zachary stumbled to respond. "How do you know my name?"

The woman looked across the street and nodded to Fat Man. "I've been expecting you.
Please come in."

131

They stepped inside together.

"My van is still parked in the street." Zachary pointed through the closed door behind him.

The woman held up her hand. "Listen."

They could hear the sound of the motorcycles pulling away from the embassy. She smiled and said, "It has been taken care of."

"I'm going to have to ask you to leave any weapons at the door. You can put your keys and wallet and belt in that basket so I can clear you through security."

Fat Man was gone; Zachary was in the hands of a black woman he didn't know, from a country he had never been to. And she knew his name. Moving from the world of leather and motorcycles to the embassy felt completely surreal. Alice in Wonderland.

He followed the woman's directions mechanically. A single security officer stood at attention beside the scanner and handed him his possessions on the other side.

"I am Maureen Kampala." The woman held out her hand to him as he came through the security gate. "Welcome to Zimbabwe."

Maureen Kampala led Zachary down a short hall to a room lavishly furnished. "Our former president hated America, but was determined to make a good impression." She motioned toward a chair. "Please, have a seat. Tea or coffee?"

"Coffee, please." Zachary couldn't relax. Their plan had gone to hell and Serena was still missing. He didn't want to think about what might have happened to her. He dropped the manila folder on the coffee table and walked to a painting hanging above the fireplace mantle. A single massive elephant, surrounded by dust dominated the center. Ears outspread, trunk raised. The creature stood at the edge of a water hole. Scrub trees, damaged by overgrazing elephants, framed the beast.

A soft voice interrupted his reverie. "Beautiful isn't it."

He spun around and stood staring.

"Serena Chavez," he replied, unbelieving. "Yes, you are." He caught her up in his arms and spun her around. She laughed then. That nagging sense of suspicion he thought he heard in her voice on the phone was gone. Far away. Another time.

Finally, he put her down and held her at arms length. "How the hell did you get here?" His voice was serious. "I thought Dead Guy had you?"

"Actually, it was Cheerio," Serena replied.

"I'm going to ring his neck," Zachary said. "At least he could have called."

"Not a chance. Cheerio, for all his endearing qualities, is entirely and completely paranoid. Wouldn't touch a cellphone. You've taken up with quite a group of outlaws." Serena rolled her eyes. "In his defense, he was busy impersonating an officer, stealing a police car, hiding said police car, keeping me out of harm's way, convincing me he was a good guy. Besides, it wouldn't be safe to talk on a cell phone and ride a motorcycle at the same time."

"I'm still going to ring his neck."

Serena pushed back from him. "You've got a whole lot of explaining to do."

Maureen Kampala entered carrying a silver tray with three cups and a matching silver carafe. "We've also got some work to do," She set the service down on the coffee table and picked up the manila folder. "May I?"

"By all means." Zachary and Serena moved to a couch where they could sit close to each other.

Serena poured the coffee while Maureen spent a few minutes skimming the contents of the folder. When Maureen looked up, her eyes were wet with tears.

Zachary Morgan felt a pang of guilt. Seeing Serena made him forget the tragedy that brought him here.

"I was there, you know," Serena spoke softly to Maureen. "I shot several hundred pictures of the flood zone. Even still, I can't believe it was the work of man. It seemed too big. Too complete. I only wished I could have seen Zimbabwe before the disaster. Here, surrounded by the marble palaces of our capitol, that feels like another planet."

"It is not so far. My younger sister and her husband were killed in this flood. Her children are with her husband's family now." Maureen did not wipe away the tears.

"I need to get back to the office and write my story, so I can roast that Michi bastard," Zachary said. "Though I'm afraid all I can do is keep running until I can find some way to get out of the country."

"That is not a problem," Maureen replied.

"I'm afraid it is. By now, my name and passport details will raise flags at every security checkpoint in the country. If the New York fireman dies, I'll be lucky if I even make it to court. Prison justice might get me long before a jury cuts me to pieces."

"But you have already left the country," Maureen countered.

Realization spread over Zachary's face. "Diplomatic immunity can only be carried so far."

"Yes. This embassy is officially Zimbabwean soil. Maybe we can help   each   other."

Chapter 54
Presidential Palace, Harare, Zimbabwe

Gideon Chipinduka greeted Stuart at the door to his private office. The security detail stood guard outside. Rigid attention.

This time Chipinduka wore a double-breasted suit and finely pressed trousers. A thin black tie rested against a starched white shirt with a silver pen. The man looked as comfortable in the full state regalia as he did grubbing around in the garden.

"It is good to see you, Mr. President." Stuart took the proffered hand. "I came as soon as I could."

"Thank you. Please come in." The president pointed to a pair of upholstered chairs opposite his desk.

Davison Chuma, already in the other chair, rose smiling to greet Stuart. "My friend, it looks as if we are thrown together once again."

They stood until the president took his chair, then settled across from him. Stuart felt a kindred connection to these men. Like himself, they had paid dearly for the restoration of their country.

"I have here, on my desk, another report which I received just this morning. An entire village outside Kanyemba was ransacked sometime last week. An old man, who was relieving himself, escaped the slaughter and managed to make it to the boma police station and raise the alarm. Of course, it was too late."

Chipinduka put on reading glasses and scanned the report. "A gang of thugs. Same story. We could kill them, but unless we took away their market, another group of men would doubtless rise to fill their places."

The president stood and walked to the window. "But we've had an unlikely break. Two sources have independently identified a

135

target. Not only do we know who is sponsoring the human trafficking, we have recently come to learn the same man was behind the destruction of the Kariba Dam.

Stuart immediately leaned forward in his chair. "What are you saying?"

"Apparently, this man invested millions in South American copper markets just before the Kariba hydroelectric supply went off-line, effectively cutting power to this region's copper mines." Chipinduka explained.

"How could anyone pull that off without being seen?"

"According to our sources, the operatives used a non-explosive demolition agent to capitalize on the dam's inherent weaknesses."

"That can't be. What kind of man would throw away that many lives just to see his stocks go up?" Stuart's jaw muscles bulged as he worked to control his anger. "Let's get him."

"As you know, the government of Zimbabwe can, officially, have no part in what I am asking you to do," he looked up from the paper and studied the faces of the men opposite, "but it will benefit our people, and it will benefit mankind."

Davison Chuma removed a netbook and logged on to a web site. "I created a website to post the man's crimes, the charges brought against him, the evidence collected and, God willing, the date and manner of his death. Only, no one will know *who* killed him." He paused and flicked through an off-line version of the site.

Stuart looked at Chuma. "Why the website? I thought we want to keep this as quiet as possible."

Chipinduka replied. "It was my idea. Any man will continue in evil until a change of heart or until it is no longer profitable or safe. We hope to illustrate to those who continue to oppress others with no voice that someone is watching them. There is justice. Evil can no longer operate under the cover of darkness. We want to bring justice and prevent injustice at the same time. That is why the death penalty is effective. Not because it is humane, but simply because it is so decisive. A man who thinks he can cut short the life of another will think twice if faced with death. The death penalty is the one horrible way a government can uphold the value of humanity and deter homicide at the same time.

"Your operation will include two reporters to provide independent documentation of the man's crimes, validating the mercenaries' rationale."

"Mercenaries?" Stuart raised his eyebrows.

"You and your team," Chipinduka replied. "The reporters will document the man's execution. We don't want to set a precedent for every rogue militia group to pick the people they like least and wipe them out. Instead, we are creating an international court of justice. It operates not only to address the suffering of our own people, but to address the suffering of the world. Every judgment given by our team must be verified by reliable sources. That is our code. This is the first time a black country has launched a black operation for the good of humanity as a whole."

The president returned to sit at his desk. "As Chuma has said before, even when it doesn't directly benefit our country, when we stand with justice, we stand with God. That is the team I want to be on."

Davison Chuma closed his netbook. "We will make an example of those whose money or position keep them from experiencing the teeth of justice. They can no longer hide behind the laws of their country, or bureaucracy of governments, or money to pay off judges and lawyers."

Stuart whistled softly. "I like it. You think this will work? I mean, will it really deter evil?"

"Yes," Chipinduka replied. "For years oppressive governments have ruled under the shadow of fear. Now, for the first time, I think, we will use fear to keep down those who would take the children of our country and sell them on the sex markets of Europe, Asia and America. Only wicked men should live in fear of punishment. This is far better than the innocent living in fear of evil."

Stuart chuckled. "Robin Hood."

Davison Chuma nodded. "Yes. Only this Mr. Hood will cut his opponents into pieces and post pictures for the world to see."

Stuart shrugged. "Very effective, though a bit gruesome. Aren't you afraid someone might find out who is behind this? It would only serve to validate the machete-wielding stereotype western media holds about Africa."

The President put the briefing on his desk. "I'm willing to take the risk. If we have learned anything from the oppression of Mwanyisa, we have learned the world does not really care about the rights of our people unless their oil or economy is involved. I will not wait for the West to approve the validity of our claim for justice. I will not even wait for the Tribunal of the Southern African Development Community. I'm tired of waiting on broken political systems."

"It is unlikely anyone would find out," Chuma said. "We have, after all, inherited from Mwanyisa some of the most advanced internet safety firewalls available on the market. Our former dictator's paranoia will serve us well."

The president turned to Stuart. "Is your team assembled?"

"At this point there are four of us. Howard Cambric, who ran logistics before, will fill that role again but will remain here. Then there is Aaron Ball, myself and Kilo."

"What of Daniel, your son-in-law?" Chipinduka asked.

"He has young children. It was my choice to keep him home. He would have come. Maybe next time."

"Good."

"We've been training, as best as we can, not knowing the operation." Stuart's hint was not lost on the president. He didn't like training blind.

"Perhaps this will help." Chipinduka reached into a drawer and pulled out a manila folder. "Here are the details of the assignment. Of course, anything can change in an operation like this."

"Yes, sir."

"And there is one more thing. If you will come with me?"

The president opened a door in his office and led Stuart back a hallway and down a set of stairs to a concrete bunker.

"Mwanyisa had an armory built underneath his house. It was, in fact, more of a museum of military hardware. He was something of a collector. It fed his lust for power." The president pushed a button and a vault door swung open.

Stuart let out a low whistle. Matching sets of every conceivable kind of weapon hung on display. It was a munitions storehouse the likes of which few had never seen. Stuart ran his hand over the wooden stock of a 9 mm Lanchester submachine gun and picked it up. "This weapon was used during World War II. It actually was a copy of a German MP 28. I wonder if Mwanyisa thought about the irony of a weapon designed after a German gun being used to defeat the Germans."

"It is fitting, don't you think?" The president chuckled.

"It looks like two of everything in here." Stuart continued to walk around the store room, studying the veritable museum of modern firearms. From pistols to machine guns, every piece was mounted above drawers holding collections of ammunition specific to that weapon. It appeared to be organized by type, with Egyptian and Polish submachine guns displayed next to each other. An adjacent section housed revolvers, another, machine guns, and so on. There were antechambers filled with absurd or unusual items used during the height of the cold war by spies, even crossbows hanging over bundles of razor-tipped arrows.

"An inventory of the armory is included in the packet I gave you. It includes everything: revolvers, swords, machine guns. Everything. As far as I know, you are the only other person who knows of this collection. It is entirely at your disposal. Select whatever you need for the operation. If there is anything else I can do…"

Stuart put the Lanchester back in its place. "Thank you."

The president nodded. "How soon can you be ready to move?"

"Twenty-four hours."

"Good. Put your men on standby." They walked out of the storeroom and waited as the vault doors closed. Then the president put his hand on Stuart Hall's shoulder. "God go with you."

Chapter 55
Baltimore Washington International Airport
Baltimore, MD

Colette Logan mailed the Senator tapes off to the Texan. As usual, she kept copies of everything. The balance of her payment had arrived in a bank account in Zurich the previous day.

Tray cried when she hugged him goodbye. She had a file on him as well.

"You will write, won't you, Lakshanya?" Tray asked, smiling sheepishly at his tears. "I was never good at stoic goodbyes."

"Of course, I'll write." She found herself uncomfortable with the lie.

She kissed him gently on the lips and checked herself through security at the Baltimore Washington International airport. Her flight left in an hour. She traveled light. Her revolver, the Rossi 351 02, would arrive ahead of her courtesy of UPS. She could have purchased another firearm in Dubai, where one could buy anything, but Colette didn't want to attract attention and she wouldn't have much time on the Arabian Peninsula.

Terminal traffic picked up. Colette found a café near her gate. She had a short layover in Munich before her connecting flight to the United Arab Emirates. From there, she would meet her contact and accept delivery of the weapon.

Her nervousness irritated her. She didn't know if she could trust an African president with her contact information; she only hoped he was more desperate to get Michi than she was. Maybe it was the caffeine. She had been careful; tediously careful, but Ciro Michi didn't take chances either.

Colette stared at the passers-by. Watching. Always watching. Michi probably intended to murder her. It was only a matter of time. She tried to convince herself she could make peace with her death if she could make some things right beforehand.

Chapter 56
Dubai, United Arab Emirates

The iconic tower of the Burg Khalifa blocked the evening sun, casting its shadow over the city to the east. Dubai, the Las Vegas of the Arabian Peninsula.

Colette Logan entered the lobby of her hotel, still in the shade of Dubai's grandest. White marble floors inlaid with black patterns spread from wall to wall and massive black columns rose to support their own sculpted designs.

Once again she played a role. Fake names. False passports. One day she would be free and would be herself, whoever that was. She stopped in front of the hotelier's counter.

"I'm here to meet with a Mr. Patel. My name is Lakshanya Brookes."

He nodded. "Just one minute." His accented English was crisp. Clear. He glanced at her flowing robes, and partially covered head. Most tourists didn't wear the headdress.

The man lifted a phone.

Colette surveyed the room from the mirror behind the counter. A bellhop by the door sported a red fez, and a maître d' stood by a pair of mammoth hand-carved ebony doors opening to the hotel restaurant. The lobby was largely empty of tourists.

"He will meet you in the private lounge. Right this way, please." The manager led her across the lobby to a courtyard sequestered by a stand of palm trees and etched glass privacy screens.

"Madam Brookes." Tinat Patel stood when she entered and held out his hand. "I'm pleased to meet you."

"Thank you for meeting me here."

"My pleasure." He remained standing until she settled herself in the chair across from him. Between them a glass table rested on four rhinoceros horns carved in stone.

"You understand I would like to engage a crew for my vessel. Secrecy is paramount. I was told you were the best in the business for this kind of acquisition."

Tinat spread his hands and shrugged. "I am at your service."

"No one must know that we have spoken. From now on, you will communicate with me through this address." She slid a card across the glass. Silver lettering on black.

He nodded. "Secrecy is my business. I will send you a password so you can browse my database. I am sure you will find it helpful in every particular. The vessel will be ready at your date and stocked with fuel and supplies. My private skeleton crew will take the vessel off-shore from Abu Dhabi and place her at anchor. They will leave before your crew is transported aboard. Leave those arrangements to me." He studied the card briefly before handing it back. Then Tinat stood and nodded toward the back. "I will leave the way I came in."

Chapter 57
Dubai, United Arab Emirates

Colette Logan logged into the secure crewmember database from her hotel room. The data base contained almost two thousand names, each vetted and carefully selected by Tinat Patel. Captains, navigators, stewards, bartenders, prostitutes and massage. It was all here. A complete listing of private staff for luxury yachts.

The boat required sixteen, but eleven were fillers. She would need to select these carefully. Mostly women, probably. Women who would not interfere with their plans. But there were five names she had to include.

Tinat Patel created his staffing service for the rich and famous. He charged ridiculous amounts of money, kept a low profile and carefully pre-checked all sources. His reputation preceded him. Most clients came through the Emirates and were people of considerable substance. People who wanted to live large and remain unknown. Some wanted fresh crews. Others wanted fresh women. Tinat organized his working prostitutes under the 'entertainment' section. All employees worked with strict confidentiality agreements, were paid handsomely for their silence, and worked hard to keep customers happy. No exceptions. Only once had an employee disappointed a customer. She had gone missing at sea. Tinat made sure there was always a bouncer—one crewmember on board to serve as enforcer. No one knew who he was, but they knew he was there. That was usually enough to keep a crew in line.

This time it would be different. Colette knew the man's price, and she had people who were willing to pay. She assured Tinat his business would not be compromised. This time, no bouncer. She would go instead, but all the names she wanted had to be enlisted from the same service. Michi insisted.

Colette gave the Zimbabwean embassy Tinat's contact information so their people could apply to the database. She only hoped Patel had already cleared the crewmembers. The man had been given a guarantee of significant cash and the promise that his livelihood would not be compromised by the operation. Colette moused over the search icon and selected it. Her fingernails made a clicking noise as she keyed in the names she'd been given. One at a time. They were there. All under false names.

Stuart Hall, Kilo Kasangula and Aaron Ball. Chief engineer, bartender, pilot. Then the reporters: Zachary Morgan and Serena Chavez. Their pictures showed up under housekeeping.

Sometime after midnight Colette made the final selections. First, she sent a copy of the names to Ciro Michi. He would be happy to know she was on the ground in Dubai and had a crew selected. The special operatives would need to get into place. Soon they would set sail for the Mediterranean to pick up Ciro Michi's gold. Michi was already in Abu Dhabi with his yacht, less than two hours away, but he would slip aboard in his own quiet way.

Chapter 58
United Arab Emirates

Since being sequestered in the Zimbabwean embassy, Zachary Morgan and Serena Chavez spent every minute together. Planning their escape from the United States under cover of diplomatic immunity consumed their time. The stress of being exposed and returned to the US government took its toll on their sleep. They flew first to the islands of St. Croix and then took a ferry to St. Vincent in the Grenadines. A private plane carried them to Brazil where they boarded a DHL flight to Cairo, Egypt.

Friends of Zimbabwe's government in the Egyptian underworld escorted Serena and Zachary the rest of the way to the Arabian Peninsula. The two arrived at last in Al Fujayrah, a town in the north-eastern corner of the United Arab Emirates. Here they met Yussif, their guide. He tucked them away in the back of his flat while he and his wife found dress and provisions for their final push into the desert. The Americans' arrival in Al Fujayrah could not have been more pleasant. Their host prattled on in broken English while his wife fussed over Serena's wardrobe. She spoke no English, but treated them like family in spite of the fact that neither joined the daily call to prayer.

Serena and Zachary would have enjoyed lingering in their company but were on a tight schedule.

Yussif woke them long before sunrise. His wife set out a simple meal of bread rolls and sweet tea. She blessed them before they mounted the waiting camels and set off into the desert. The sun rose several hours after Al Fujayrah disappeared. Around them, from the distant peak of Jabal Yibir in the north down toward the truncial coast along the Persian Gulf, the desert revealed no hint of vegetation. The entire panoramic view boasted a mélange of brown, red and gold.

Their guide led them unerringly to an oasis hidden in a narrow canyon tucked between endless folds of sand. Here the bare rock displayed softer colors than the surrounding desert and provided a respite from the choking dry wind. Yussif left two camels and a GPS—the new way to travel in the desert—before returning to Al Fujayrah. He told them to wait in the oasis until nightfall, when they would make the final part of their journey. The next morning they would meet the African team.

Wind and sand carved away at stone over the millennia leaving bizarre shapes and culverts where Serena and Zachary made day camp. The sun rose as surreal waves of heat danced around the canyon.

But here, hidden in a depression, seven palm trees shaded an ancient spring. Water spilled fresh and cold from the rock face forming a pool. A profound silence rested on the place. Serena and Zachary lay in the shade of the palm fronds, wishing it could last forever. They slept until the heat stirred them. Serena slipped out of the robe Yussif's wife had given her and waded into the emerald pool. Zachary followed and the two swam and held each other and warmed themselves on the rocks.

When they were hungry, Serena pulled a cloth bundle from their pack and spread it out in the shade. They ate dried dates and pistachios and drank water flavored with a hint of citrus fruit. Then they lay in the shade and slept again until long shadows of night and the cold crept in and woke them for their journey.

Chapter 59
Abu Dhabi, United Arab Emirates

Only a few ports in the world offered boat slips specifically designed to accommodate super yachts of *Josie*'s size. Around the time of the great Etihad Formula One races, the slips of Abu Dhabi were all rented and fans wealthy enough to own a boat, or lucky enough to be invited, could watch the races from their own decks. After the event, fans drank and danced and partied while the sparkling lights of the great city threw reflections across the water.

Today, the *Josie* was alone with engines silent. A temporary crew had seen to the final provisions of fuel and fresh water while box vans drove down the pier to unload food orders. Here and there, sightseers gawked at the massive yacht and speculated on what someone must do for a living to afford such luxury.

Ciro Michi wore a white butcher's apron over an embroidered chef's coat. He carried a waxed box of fresh figs on board and disappeared inside the ship. He hated sneaking around, but as of yet, no one knew who owned the *Josie*, and Michi intended to keep it that way. He purposed to avoid the spotlight in commercial ports where ignorant spectators were inclined to be more curious and less deferential to men of great wealth. He would remain a 'chef' until the temporary crew disembarked and the real crew came aboard. None of that would happen until after the boat left port. His secretary had hired a local pilot to take the ship away from the activity of the Abu Dhabi into the Persian Gulf where the transfer of crews would take place. The existing crew would be ferried to shore on two separate tenders, each to a different location. Anyone who might wonder about the chef would assume he was aboard the other tender. Only then would Michi lose his cover.

Then he could return to Italy and pick up his gold.

Michi opened the door to a walk-in cooler and placed the figs on a polished aluminum shelf. The rest of the grocery items would arrive any minute, so he made his way to the galley were he retrieved a glass bottle of water from an industrial grade fridge and settled down to wait.

Chapter 60
Desert, United Arab Emirates

Stuart arranged for them to travel by camel. A nice touch which added panache to their cover. Stuart wanted to meet in the desert outside of Abu Dhabi. It had been more complicated, but he was determined to stay inconspicuous. The only sound during their cold night journey across the desert was the squeak of leather and hempen saddles and the occasional grunt of a camel. Upon arrival, Baba, their host, sent a herd boy to tend the mounts. He let them wash and ushered them inside the tent for sweet Turkish coffee. After serving them he returned to stand vigil outside. The awning of the nomad's tent opened to the brilliant spray of fading stars.

Stuart, Kilo and Aaron waited inside until a gentle cough from Baba outside told them others were approaching.

The approaching camels silhouetted black against a purple sunrise that spilled over the endless sand dunes. Two riders dismounted and handed their leads to the herd boy.

Stuart was impressed. The Americans seemed comfortable enough out here. Most Westerners—Americans especially—did a poor job of relaxing in unfamiliar places. These two even wore traditional Arab dress.

Baba, bowing and salaaming, led the new arrivals to a canvas wash basin beneath a palm.

"Welcome." Stuart stepped forward. "I trust you traveled well. I'm Stuart Hall."

"Yes, thank you." Serena shook his hand. "Serena Chavez. This is Zachary Morgan." Serena gestured to the tent. "Nice place."

Zachary smiled. "She always liked camping."

Stuart chuckled. Maybe these Americans wouldn't be so hard to work with. "Shall we?" He gestured toward the tent.

After greetings around the circle, the group settled themselves on low cushions arranged around the center pole of the tent.

Their host laid a simple breakfast of fruits and more coffee.

"Turkish coffee…black as death, sweet as love and strong as hell," Aaron smiled, "or something like that."

They ate without talking, embracing the serenity of Baba's hospitality. Except for the pomegranates, the fruits were dried but retained more moisture than the rubbery leathery specimens carried by American grocers. Baba then passed around a pastry that smelled strangely citrus.

"Delicious." Serena licked her fingers. "I wonder what it is."

"Women are so hard to please these days." Zachary rolled his eyes playfully. "She has been complaining the entire trip."

A pleasant ripple of laughter followed and the party seemed to relax. Baba poured streams of hot coffee into the glass cups set in silver holders and smiled at their conversation, understanding nothing.

After breakfast, the party leaned back on cushions and chatted until Stuart brought the meeting to point.

"President Chipinduka has given me a summary of charges against our target. Not only is the man heavily involved in sex trafficking from the central African region, but our sources inform us his trafficking network extends from Vietnam to California. The man is responsible for the sale of over twenty-five thousand people.

"Other charges against him deal directly with financing the operation to destroy Kariba Dam. That alone resulted in the death of millions. If for some reason any one of you feels this man does not deserve to die, now is your time to beg out. Of course, for

152

security reasons, you'll have to stay here until the operation is complete." He looked from face to face around the circle. "I ask because he *is* going to die, and his death will be unpleasant. It must serve as an example for others who think they can pursue a life of depravity without facing the kind of violence they visit on others."

Stuart settled his cup back into the silver tray and continued. "In just a few hours we'll be ferried onto his yacht when he swaps out his existing crew. Once we're on board, there's no turning back."

He turned to Serena. "I don't mean to stereotype, but are you prepared for this? I have a daughter not much younger than you. If I had been given the choice, I would not have allowed a woman to join an operation like this. It won't be easy to watch."

The weak lamplight shaded the contours of Serena's face. For a long minute she didn't speak. "I was in Africa," she said. "I followed the Zambezi River from the Kariba Gorge down to the Indian Ocean." Serena stopped and stared out the open doorway at the growing light of morning, groping for words. "I've seen a lot. I can't stand suffering," she turned and stared right into Stuart's eyes, "but whatever you have planned for this man is not bad enough."

Chapter 61
Mediterranean Sea
Aboard the *Josie*

After leaving the United Arab Emirates and swapping out her crew, the *Josie* rounded the Arabian Peninsula, crossed the Suez Canal and entered the Mediterranean.

For the first time in months, Michi had a vent for his rage. He finished with the woman and now she sat, tied hand and foot to a chair. Michi fished through his pocket for a packet of cigarettes and lit one, drawing the smoke deep into his lungs before walking to the girl and blowing it into her face.

"It isn't your fault, you see." He spoke in English so she would understand him. She was young and her skin was clean.

Her fear delighted him. Michi gently pushed back the hair from her face and whispered into her ear. "I can promise you; this is going to hurt you more than it is going to hurt me." He laughed at his own joke.

He waved the burning end in front of her face and smiled when she winced. "Maybe, if you scream loud enough to satisfy me, I will let you live."

Chapter 62
Sorrento, Italy

Traveling at eighteen knots, the *Josie* covered almost 200 miles a day. Four days after leaving the Arabian Peninsula, she slipped into Sorrento's harbor after nightfall.

A single boat plied the waters between yacht and harbor. The sky above Sorrento turned deep blue. Michi watched from the companionway outside the pilot house as the fishing boat sidled up against the gull wing loading doors on the port side of the yacht's bow. Lights from the two-hundred-forty foot *Josie* dwarfed the fishing boat. A loading arm extended from the cargo bay and dropped a hook to the man standing beside the last of four pallets.

The fisherman grabbed the hook and fastened it to the pallet harness. The winch whined and the pallet slowly lifted. The fisherman waited for the load to clear before moving back to the wheel. He nodded up at the man on the deck of the yacht.

Michi nodded in return. He watched the fisherman pull away as the loading arm retracted and the gull wing doors sealed shut. He knew his crew would be stowing the cargo as per instructions.

Colette Logan came up beside him. "All is in order. Ready when you are."

"Almost." His eyes never left the fishing vessel. He withdrew a remote from his pocket and waited until the boat moved farther off. Then he depressed the button.

A dull crack echoed as explosives ripped a hole in the bottom of the boat. Then a flash of light followed in the helm where a secondary device instantly killed the fisherman. It was not brighter than the flash from a camera. Insignificant to any watching.

Though out of sight, Michi knew the boat was sinking.

"Now we are ready," he said.

He turned to Colette Logan and gestured toward the water. "Here is a lesson for you, Colette. Always be thorough. I don't like loose ends." He chuckled. "I even have a life insurance policy with a talented young man."

Colette shot him a quizzical look.

"Yes." Michi paused to button the front of his sport coat and adjust his tie. "If I die, whoever is responsible will be paid in full."

Chapter 63
Mediterranean Sea

Josie settled into a cruising speed of 25 knots. With a beam just under thirty-three feet, she cut through the calm waters of the Mediterranean with ease. Ciro Michi sunned himself on the party deck under the communications tower. Two female crew members provided scenery. One lay next to him in the sun while the other cooled herself in the pool. Logan picked them carefully. Both according to Michi's taste. One obsidian black. One white.

Colette Logan entered the pilot house forward and below of where the mob boss rested and walked directly to Aaron Boll. "Expect visitors at 10:30. Five of them."

Aaron was immediately concerned. "You didn't tell us about this."

"Because I didn't know," Colette replied.

"Who?"

"I imagine a special security squad." She glanced at the digital time display under the heavily tinted windows. "They arrive in ten minutes or less."

"How long have you known about this?" Aaron was angry. Accusing.

"Twelve minutes," she replied.

"Damn." Aaron began scanning the horizon. "This changes everything."

"Yes. Can you still do it?" she asked.

Aaron looked at her. Realized she was afraid. He reached out to touch her arm. "I'm sorry I snapped at you. I don't know what this means. You'll have to tell Stuart and Kilo."

#

From the bridge Aaron had radar on the chopper almost as soon as Colette told him about it. It came in fast and low. The sophisticated instrumentation in the pilot house had been tracking the helicopter before, but Aaron hadn't noticed it. He made a mental note not to make the same mistake twice. Precisely ten minutes later the thump of chopper blades pounded out of the sky and a black aircraft settled on the foredeck helipad.

Doors opened and five female guards disembarked. They unloaded a single case of gear and the chopper lifted off without the pilot breaking radio silence. Within minutes it disappeared into the horizon.

"What the hell?" Aaron spoke softly, even though they were alone on the bridge.

Colette followed his question. "Michi doesn't care if women watch him with his whores. He probably fancies men would get distracted."

Colette Logan left to see to their accommodation, though the security team moved like they had been fully briefed on the superyacht's layout.

The guards walked down one of the two companionways that led from the helipad past the pilothouse. Aaron said a nasty word under his breath but smiled and waved as they walked past the open door. Not a single one returned his greeting.

"Nice folks," he muttered. Stuart wasn't going to like this.

Chapter 64
Mediterranean Sea, North of Egypt

Stuart stared out the deeply recessed porthole, watching nothing. The security detail made it impossible for his team to meet. They devised a note passing system that served the purpose, but it was crude and dangerous.

A man like Ciro Michi spent his life making enemies and didn't trust anyone. Such a sentiment would likely have been communicated to Michi's security firm. Consequently, the security detail also wouldn't know where a threat was most likely to originate. He moved over to the desk in his cabin and sat down. As far as Michi was concerned, threats were as likely to come from sea as from aboard ship. This meant the guards had a lot to watch. A security team often feared what they couldn't see more than what they could.

Stuart drew a rough sketch of the yacht and considered the guard's placement. He marked these with an 'x'. One guard always stayed with Michi who confined himself to his suite or the top sun deck. The bridge seemed to attract the most attention. Two guards remained there, where they could monitor the navigation and radar equipment. Stuart put two marks on the bridge and a third on the foredeck helipad. This guard kept a visual on the ship's perimeter. Not a bad plan, he mused. Stuart put his pen down to study the drawing.

What bothered Stuart most was the size of the team. Five guards seemed like a paltry number for a yacht this size. He clenched his fist and relaxed it. Either Michi was arrogant enough to feel safe, or there was something Stuart was missing.

Because of his uncertainty, Stuart wanted to have the security problem wrapped up before they passed through the Suez. The long isolated banks of the canal made him nervous. He had no way of knowing what plans Michi made for himself or his gold, so Stuart made plans of his own.

The master suite on *Josie* covered the entire third level of the superyacht. The bedroom sat above and behind the pilothouse with windows on three sides. Behind the master cabin was an office, his and her bathrooms and an expansive lounge. Beyond the foyer, sliding glass doors opened to a private deck toward the stern. A stairway rose from the lounge of the master suite to the upper level where a deck surrounded a grand table for al fresco dining. Elaborate shading offered a place to watch the ocean or those on the mahogany dance floor. Toward the bow, a sunning deck wrapped around three sides of a plunge pool.

Michi sent his evening entertainment back to her own chamber. Apart from his guard in the corner, he preferred to sleep alone. Michi rang for refreshments.

Kilo arrived with a silver tray: Vodka in freshly squeezed orange juice and a covered platter.

Michi lifted the juice from the proffered tray. The girl made him thirsty. The waiter set the platter on a night stand. Michi handed back the empty glass and Kilo lifted the silver cover revealing a white plate with folded card. On it was a single word, type-written in black ink.

Kariba.

Michi startled. He raised a hand to the guard standing in the corner.

She turned toward him, but Colette Logan slipped in behind and brought her revolver down hard.

The guard crumpled to the floor. Kilo's knife flashed from the sheath on his leg, the tip of its blade touching the soft skin under Michi's chin.

Colette retrieved the guard's radio. Kilo pulled the woman's weapon from under her body, and checked her pulse.

#

Stuart glanced at his watch. It wouldn't be long before the guards' next radio check.

He moved aft through the crew accommodations to reach the engine room. As usual, the security guard assigned to crew quarters followed. He made a point of checking the engine room every two hours. The massive M71's were nothing like the tractor engines he used to monkey with on the farm. They looked like huge generators but ran whisper quiet. Thankfully the engine room monitoring systems were fairly intuitive. Stuart's background with pumps and irrigation certainly helped. He had a workable understanding of the various systems.

A color coded chart hung above the print manuals on the chief engineer's desk. With all pipes labeled, a few hours orientation served to give him an understanding of the basics. A centralized flat screen monitored the Naiad stabilizers, the bilge and firefighting system, and wastewater treatment. The vessel also had an oil and water separator to treat discharge water in an effort to minimize the superyacht's pollution footprint. All valves could be adjusted from the touch screen.

Stuart only needed to know enough about systems to look convincing. Carrying his clip board with him, he walked around the engine room making meaningless notations. He did his best to be boring and act unconcerned by the guard's company. Boring people are the hardest to watch.

The security guard stood by the door watching. Stuart had no way of knowing if she had special combat skills. His best chance was to catch her by surprise. He knew the danger of underestimating her or using less force because she was a woman.

He stopped at a dial showing the operating temperature and tapped

161

on the glass. The needle floated well below red, but Stuart frowned and glanced at his clipboard. Then he tapped the glass again. The security guard noticed his concern and moved in to see.

"Damn it," Stuart said. The guard stared at the dial. "Here," Stuart shoved his clipboard at the woman, "hold this." The guard, surprised, took the clipboard and watched as Stuart knelt to follow the thermostat's cable to its sensor.

The guard leaned in closer. "Is there a problem?" The woman's English was good, though it had a decided German lilt.

"We're running too hot." Stuart knelt over the blue circulator pump among a jumble of pipes, each marked with a directional arrow. "Pass me the tape." He pointed to a roll of silver duct tape on a work bench behind her. She hesitated, then picked it up and handed it to him. Both hands were full.

Stuart grabbed the woman's arm as she was moving toward him with the tape and, using her own momentum, pulled her hard into a pipe. She grunted as her face made contact with metal. With one hand Stuart pushed the weapon strap off her shoulder sending the submachine gun clattering to the floor with his clipboard.

Stuart twisted the girl's arm hard to keep her off balance and pushed his Colt Anaconda into her face. He selected the Colt from the dictator's stash because it was chambered for the .44 Magnum rounds and was considered one of the most accurate revolvers ever made. Though the six-inch barrel was longer than convenient for inconspicuous packing, it had a presence which he hoped would make firing unnecessary. Bottom line: he didn't want to make any noise, but if he pulled the trigger, he wanted his mark dead.

The stunned woman stared at the stainless steel weapon pressed against her cheek bone and decided the Italian upstairs wasn't worth dying for.

Stuart motioned for her to lie on the ground where he put his knee on her neck and pressed the barrel of his Colt against the back of her head. With his free hand he unclipped her radio and threw it across the floor before grabbing the tape. He bound her hands and mouth and hobbled her feet behind her.

"Handy stuff, this." Stuart waved the roll of tape in front of her face. He crouched and smiled at her wide, pretty eyes. "Sorry luv, you were in the way." He rolled the guard onto her side and unfastened her Kevlar vest. Her eyes grew wide as he worked the vest off her shoulders.

"Relax. I'm just making sure you don't have anything hiding under here I don't know about. He gave her a friendly pat on the rump before dragging her around behind the engine, so she wouldn't be seen.

Two down. Three to go.

#

Colette Logan immediately went into Michi's office in the master suite and, using the ship's phone, made direct calls to crew members requesting they report immediately to the mess hall for a briefing.

With the exception of Kilo and Aaron the entire crew reported to the area by the time she arrived. Zachary and Serena, too, mixed easily with the rest of them making banal conversation while they waited for Colette to begin. As manager, she carried significant clout among the crew. Stuart came in moments after and gave her a discreet nod.

Colette moved to the front of the room and the conversation fell silent.

"Security has asked for our assistance in a routine sweep. They expect it to take only a few minutes of our time. I know some of you are off duty, so this shouldn't interfere with your responsibilities. Because our guest is already asleep, there shouldn't be any noticeable interruption in our service."

She picked up a glass of champagne sitting next to her. One of the crew handed around a tray of glasses. Colette waited until everyone had a glass except Stuart.

"The champagne is a small thank you from our guest. I figured I would take this occasion to pass along his thanks for a job well done so far." Colette paused and made eye contact with those around her. The girl with the burns all over her body sat in the corner without removing her sunglasses. The others ignored her. They felt relieved that the boss picked her. Maybe his appetites were satisfied.

Colette continued. "I, too, want to commend you for your work so far." She raised her champagne and the others followed suit. "Cheers," she said.

The crew emptied their glasses and a few patted each other on the back.

Colette again called them to attention. "If you could report to your quarters now, the security team will commence with their sweep, and we'll have you back to work in a few minutes."

The crew hurried out. Kilo used a lower dose of methaqualone in the crew's champagne than he had for Michi. Though some of the crew made it onto their beds, a few fell on the floor of their cabins as the tranquilizer took effect.

Stuart helped Zachary and Serena to their bunks. The two had taken the drink in order to avoid suspicion. Slumped onto their bed, Zachary grabbed Stuart's sleeve and whispered, "Next time, remind me not to drink the Kool-Aid."

#

Kilo carried the tray of three drinks into the bridge. Two security guards stood watch where Aaron worked. Stuart suggested the security detail were mercenaries for hire spawned by the German underworld. International security was big business. The women might have been considered pretty under better circumstances. Most had distinctive Aryan features, but their battle dress uniforms did little to flatter. Both women carried the short-barreled black Heckler and Koch MP5A3. The German 9mm submachine gun first saw service with border patrol agents along the Iron Curtain. Unlike the A2, the A3 had a telescoping stock which improved its versatility in close-range combat. A three-setting, selector switch rested above the trigger on the left side.

Aaron bent over the airplane-like radar and navigation consoles keeping track of other ships and aircraft in the vicinity. He was not going to have a repeat of their previous surprise. Though the guards spoke English, they didn't talk much and only communicated with each other in German. Aaron, however, made it a point to natter on about nothing while they were around. Treat them like guests.

Kilo coughed politely to get his attention. "Your drinks, Captain."

"These ladies are good, eh?" Aaron nodded toward the women who stood near the doors on opposite sides of the room. Both armed and stoically uninvolved in the mundane. "They must be bored out of their mind by now." He gestured to the control suite around him. "It is pretty exciting stuff, staring at a bunch of displays and readouts all day."

Kilo chuckled. "Is that why you ordered three?"

"As a matter of fact, it is. A night-cap with a couple of ladies who let me do all the talking sounds like just what the doctor ordered." Aaron pointed to the guard closest to Kilo and noticed a shift in her stance, a break in the reserve. Keep going Kilo, he thought.

Kilo took the drink off the tray and handed it to her. "A bastard, compliments of the captain."

The guard took the drink with one hand and stared at it, uncertain what to do next. Her other hand still rested on her weapon.

"If you don't drink it," Aaron said, "then I'll be forced to drink them all myself, which won't do much to improve my driving." Aaron chuckled at his own joke. "But, alas, ship rules state I have to stick with virgins." He lifted his drink and laughed again. "Such a pity."

Kilo walked the second drink to the other guard and pressed it into her hand. The odds were improving. "Good night, sir."

Kilo knew before he left that the women were not going to drink. On his way out, Kilo stumbled and bumped up against the first guard who still held her drink. The amber liquid splashed on her uniform and Kilo reached instinctively for his towel. As he stepped in closer to clean up the mess, he reached over and slipped her selector to 'safe.' In a flash Kilo stepped behind and had his towel around the woman's neck, lifting her completely off the ground. She dropped the drink, sending glass shattering across the floor. She found her weapon and instinctively pulled the trigger. Nothing. She swung the weapon over her head to hit her assailant, but Kilo held her high enough that her efforts were useless.

Aaron moved toward the guard near him. As she brought up her weapon, Aaron kicked her leg at the knee, breaking it inward. On the floor she swerved the MP5 toward him and would have taken a shot but Aaron's boot came down hard on her fingers.

For a few long seconds the guard lay on the floor staring wide-eyed at her leg jutting at an impossible angle. Scalding pain triggered waves of nausea. She screamed.

Aaron dove for the MP5 as the guard on the heli pad sprinted to the port side door to see what was happening. Glancing in she saw a guard still hanging from Kilo's towel—face red and eyes bulging. She turned away and sprinted down the companionway, calling for reinforcements on her radio, unaware that she was the last one.

Stuart was waiting. He threw open a companionway door in front of her, stopping her cold. She landed in a dazed heap on the ground. Stuart stepped out. "I'm terribly sorry." He reached down to help her up. Always the gentleman. She gave him a surprised look when she saw the weapon in her face. He hauled her up and hustled her toward the pilothouse.

Stuart winced when he saw the woman's leg. She passed out. The first guard, happy to be breathing, sat stewing in her bonds with a band of silver tape over her mouth.

Stuart pushed his catch toward Aaron who tied her up beside the others. "Gentlemen; the boat is ours."

#

Gertie Haas' head throbbed and the duct tape pinched her skin. She glanced at the red numbers of the digital clock. She had been here almost five hours. The discomfort in her bladder indicated a profound need. The man wasn't coming back. Gertie closed her eyes. Why should something so natural take so much concentration? She took several deep breaths and finally felt her bladder relax and the warm flush between her legs.

Gertie began to rock back and forth until she flopped over on her side. Painful cramps seared the back of her legs. Gasping from pain, she wiggled her way away from her own slippery mess toward the wall. It was then Gertie saw the black shut-off valve a few inches off the floor. The fire in her legs increased and began to spread up into her lower back. The cramps and restraints combined to feed a growing claustrophobia she had never before experienced.

Pushing back the pain, Gertie took a minute to breathe, to center herself. Then, twisting as hard as she could, she raised her leg to the round shut-off valve until she felt it bump against the emergency beacon strapped to her calf. Carefully, she wrenched her body until the handle depressed the button.

Her legs dropped back on the ground as the pain continued to spread. But the silent homing beacon had been activated. A signal transmitting to headquarters.

Chapter 65
Egyptian Territorial Waters

The coast of Egypt came into view early that morning and the Mediterranean suddenly swarmed with boats. As they neared Port Said, mammoth container ships and oil tankers mingled indiscriminately with local feluccas, which plied the water near the entrance to the Suez Canal, selling produce to smaller vessels.

Aaron Boll studied the electronic displays and saw something he hadn't noticed before. The console showed a single repeating transmission. He studied it, trying to figure out what he was seeing.

Then it dawned on him. "Dammit!" He grabbed the ship's phone. Stuart picked up on the third ring.

"Stuart, we have a problem. I've intercepted a signal transmission originating from on board. Looks like an emergency locator beacon. Very low frequency."

"Check the guards first. The crew should still be unconscious." Aaron slammed down the phone and sprinted toward the master suite.

Chapter 66
Engine Room, *Josie*

Stuart smelled urine as soon as he entered the room. He flicked on lights and ran toward the guard.

"Where is it?" He ripped the duct tape off her mouth.

She shook her head.

"Either you tell me or I go looking." He moved toward her and started a thorough pat down. She tried to twist away from him as he worked his way down her body. Her pants were still wet but he ignored it and probed deeper. He didn't have time to be polite. Just below the woman's knee he felt something. Using the hook on the back of his knife, he cut open her pant leg up to her thigh.

The beacon was the size of a credit card but thicker. He sawed through the webbed strap and stood up.

"How long has this been transmitting?"

She glared defiantly at Stuart. "Kiss my ass."

"No thanks. I need to find the rest of these. I'm guessing you all carry one."

Stuart stalked from the room and pitched the transmitter overboard. That should throw them off a bit, he thought, until we can give them something else to chase.

Chapter 67
Germany

Freda Klein saw the shortwave signal exactly thirteen seconds after Gertie activated the beacon. One minute later she put out the call for a back-up team to investigate. The request was routed through the security firm's London dispatch and relayed to a branch office on the Island of Crete.

Montrose took the call. "Ya?"

"We have an emergency transmission from your quadrant." The dispatchers tone was accusing.

Montrose took his feet off the counter and spun his chair around to look at the transponder behind him. "Yes, I see that." He cursed himself for not paying attention. "This looks like one of yours. How long have you been receiving this transmission?"

"Less than three minutes. Do you have a team available to investigate?"

"We do." Montrose pressed the alarm bell to activate the branch back-up team.

"We are still waiting for satellites to triangulate an exact position," Freda Klein said.

Montrose pulled up the company's website and typed his password. A few clicks later he was staring at a black and red digitized map showing the position of the company's satellites and a greyed out area indicating the possible location of the signal beacon. "We have another satellite coming overhead in fifteen seconds." Montrose took out a notepad. "Tell me what you know."

"Based on the pre-mission briefing, I expect the signal is coming from a vessel near Port Said, Egypt. Our client, however, refused to provide specific details on vessel specifications or itinerary," Klein said.

"Got a fix," Montrose chimed in. "The signal is just off the coast of Egypt, north and West of Port Said. A team is on the way."

Chapter 68
New York, New York

Judge Selma Watson-Jones pulled reading glasses from a beaded case and set them carefully on the end of her nose. She was in the office before it got light, and she hoped to get her paperwork finished early. After all, even the honorable Judge Selma Watson-Jones was entitled to a manicure, and she wanted it done before she visited her daughter.

The District Attorney for New York County was responsible for most of the piles on her desk.

Judge Selma sighed. It was so much reading. Most of it desperately boring. Complaints filed because of delayed hearings. Another request for a grand jury investigation into corruption charges in the mayor's office—usually politically motivated, and usually right about the money.

She picked through the stack, selecting the most interesting and sprinkling these through the pile. The ritual worked ever since middle school. Even in high school when faced with a choice between *The Scarlet Letter* and her Latin primer, she started with Latin first.

After three boring petitions, Judge Selma got to a Memorandum Request for a Grand Jury Hearing prepared by Derek Hunsinger, DA.

She pushed the glasses farther up her nose and leaned back in her chair. Finally, something interesting.

The memo outlined a formal request for the grand jury to serve in its investigative capacity—a fact-finding mission which usually ended in a request for an indictment. The district attorney listed the prime suspect as one Zachary Morgan of the *New York Times* who apparently ran amok and now faced felony charges of arson, murder and criminal homicide.

173

Selma had seen the news and expected the case would come across her desk. Once again, she would be thrown into the spotlight as she presided. In this case, the hearing was scheduled simply because a trail had gone cold and the investigators needed access to legal documents or leverage to make reluctant witnesses talk.

It was a legal formality, but formalities were important and Judge Selma Watson-Jones believed in them. The publicity was a perk.

Chapter 69
Mediterranean Sea
5 miles north of Port Said, Egypt

The chopper hovered right on top of a signal. The security team scanned the water beneath while the pilot flew a search grid over the area.

"What do you see?" the pilot asked.

"Nothing. Absolutely nothing." The team leader twisted his neck again to scan the water below from the passenger seat of the aircraft. "Let's not waste any more time. We need to find the ship."

"What if we missed her?"

"If she's down there somewhere, we're too late to do her any good."

Static cracked across their headsets and dispatch broke in. "The last four transmitters just went hot."

"How far?" the team leader asked.

"Just a few minutes."

Chapter 70
Port Said, Egypt

The naval authority in Port Said had already been contacted. All necessary documentation was sent via the ship's fax machine. The *Josie* sat idling with a host of other boats awaiting their turn to enter the Suez Canal.

In the bridge all eyes were on the radar. They didn't know exactly from where the helicopter would be coming or how soon, but they knew it would be coming. Of the four guards remaining on board, only one managed to activate her signal beacon, but they'd found the rest of the transmitters.

At exactly 11:23 Aaron noticed the first green blip on his screen, moving in fast from the northwest.

#

"Approaching Target at nine o'clock. ETA one minute." The pilot slowed. A guard slid back the chopper's side door and braced himself in the opening. Four other soldiers crouched behind. The chopper banked hard, sending up a spray of water from below and came in on the starboard side of their target. The pilot pushed a button and the red light on the bulkhead behind him turned green. "Time to go." He hovered four feet over the helipad of the massive yacht.

Five men in black fatigues dropped to secure the perimeter of the helipad before touch down. One guard stayed near the helipad. In seconds, the rest dispersed, working the yacht in teams of two, leapfrogging from one door to another in a fast-paced, precision search. Gun metal gleamed in the Mediterranean sun.

The first team paused outside the bridge before smashing through the door.

176

Four men on the bridge hit the floor and lay with hands covering their heads. A woman standing by an interior entrance let out a shriek and fled the room. A guard followed and kicked her feet out from underneath. She fell hard. Taking her by the hair and a fistful of shirt, he dragged her back to the bridge and dropped her on the floor next to the others. He waved the barrel of his weapon menacingly around the room. "Where is the security team?"

The silence was broken only by the woman's stifled cries.

The guard pushed his weapon into the small of the woman's back. "I will only ask one more time. Where is my security team?"

One man peeked up from under his hands. "I don't know what you are talking about. We don't have a security team here."

The two other guards returned from their search. The last one onto the bridge shook his head.

"Who is the owner of this vessel?" The guard pushed his weapon harder into the woman until she let out another gasp.

"It is me. I'm the owner. Leave her alone." A gray-haired Asian man attempted to get up while keeping his hands on his head.

The guard looked at him quizzically then turned to one of his team. "Go find the beacons."

The man shouldered his weapon and removed a receiver from his pocket. He turned on the device and walked out of the bridge, following the signal to its source.

Four minutes later he was back.

"The beacons are attached to the anchor chain. Let's get out of here."

"Damn!" The team leader signaled to his men. Without a word, they filed out of the bridge, boarded the chopper and lifted off over the water.

#

On the deck of the *Josie* two pair of binoculars were trained on the chopper as it swooped in over the sea. Aaron and Colette lay in swim suits soaking up sun behind dark sunglass, casually watching the chopper arrive and land on the helipad of a neighboring oceangoing research vessel, their own weapons hidden but in easy reach. If the chopper had landed on their yacht, they would have the positional advantage. When the chopper settled down on a neighboring vessel, the two got up and stood at the rail. Normal human curiosity. The two gawked a few minutes before returning to the deck chairs. After a tortuous ten minutes, the helicopter lifted off and passed directly over the *Josie.* Colette waved. The shadow of the aircraft momentarily blinked across the sun and disappeared, flying back the way it had come.

Aaron turned and looked at Colette. "Where did you learn to scuba dive?"

"Cinnamon Bay, St. John, United States Virgin Islands." Colette smiled. "Nice place."

Aaron leaned back on his chair and relaxed for the first time. He let out a sigh, "We should do this more often." Then he reached across and grabbed her hand. "Nice swimming. I think we owe you one."

Colette laughed. For a fleeting instant, she was just another tourist in the Mediterranean. But the moment passed, innocence disappeared long ago.

Chapter 71
Suez Canal, Egypt

The *Josie* retraced her path through the Suez, heading south toward the Red Sea.

Once they slept off the champagne, some of the crew whispered about the disappearance of security personnel. But because of the superyacht's layout, it was easy enough to keep the crew away from Michi's suite and Colette had hinted that Michi may not even be on board. A rich man like that probably had important meetings he was required to fly in and out for. A helicopter might have come and gone while they were sleeping. So long as they were getting paid, what should they care?

Zachary and Serena moved freely. They came up early enough to see the twin minarets of the Al Salam Mosque slip past them in Port Said. They continued the charade of being crewmembers during the passage through the Suez Canal. Zachary downloaded his work email onto his phone. For the first time since the fire, Morgan could think about his old life.

He scanned through a thousand messages. Several from Philip Monroe, his editor and boss. Zachary read in chronological order.

First Monroe demanded Zachary Morgan present what evidence he had accumulated. Morgan wondered exactly how a person with no tact got to be in charge of the newspaper. Monroe was positively caustic. He demanded independent evidence to corroborate this story about an Italian mob boss being responsible for the destruction of a dam no one had heard about until it crumbled and swept away several million people.

The second email asked him to call right away.

The third was the shortest. The subject line read: Urgent.

The body contained three words: *You are fired.* Under his brief

179

note, was a forwarded email from the New York police outlining in some detail the allegations against him.

Zachary swore and tossed his phone onto the bunk. "I was afraid of that."

"What's the matter?" Serena asked.

"The fireman is dead. I'm wanted by the state of New York. My employment has officially been terminated."

Serena listened. What to say?

"I don't think I can ever go back," Zachary said. "What life do I have left?"

Chapter 72
Red Sea
Due east of Luxor (Valley of the Kings)

After they entered the canal Stuart arranged to drop the guard with a broken leg at a hotel along the shores of Bitter Lake. She had been coming in and out of consciousness through most of their trip down the Suez. The other guards were being held on board. Stuart planned to drop them off on a deserted stretch of the Yemeni coast. By the time they made it to civilization, the *Josie* would be long gone.

The rest of the crew was unloaded without explanation in El Suweis on the southern end of the Suez Canal, their payment routed through Tinat Patel's staffing service.

The boss, apparently drunk, did not appear to see them off, but then they hadn't expected him to. In all, theirs had been a lucrative voyage from the United Arab Emirates into the Mediterranean and back again. Twice through the Suez. The manager assured them they would receive strong letters of recommendation for their work aboard the *Josie*. The employer had even been kind enough to pay for the short flights back to Abu Dubai in the United Arab Emirates where they could book their next gig on the vessels of the rich and famous.

The *Josie* came to rest in the Red Sea several miles off the coast of Egypt east of the city of Bur Safaga. The yacht tender from the *Josie* made landfall just south of the city. They off-loaded a casket and trumped up from the beach to a delivery van parked alongside the coastal highway.

"We're all set." Aaron patted the side of the van.

"Where did you get this?" Zachary asked.

"A loaner," Aaron replied, with half a grin.

Zachary and Serena climbed in back with Aaron. The crude casket contained the alive but sedated Ciro Michi. Kilo drove like a drunk around potholes and Stuart navigated their way around the township sprawl that ringed Bur Safaga.

Serena braced herself as the van careened over a rough spot in the road. "What's to keep the guards from talking?"

"They will, but we'll be long gone. As it is, they'll have a rough time explaining how they got to be in an uptight, foreign country without passports, wearing nothing but military fatigues."

"Hopefully their bumps and bruises will remind them to pick more worthy men to guard the next time," Zachary suggested.

"I'm going to have a few bumps and bruises of my own to remind me of Kilo's driving," Serena added.

Sometime after midnight, the delivery van passed through the city of Qena where they crossed the Nile and followed the west bank south toward Luxor. After four hours of Egyptian roads, Kilo turned onto a dirt track. According to Aaron, they were doing a night tour near the Valley of the Kings. Through the windows they could see the peak of al-Qurn, vaguely pyramidal in shape, against the backdrop of stars. Bouncing over a series of tracks, they wound their way into the Theban hills.

Aaron briefed them. They would spend the day hidden among the hills before returning to the coast. When Aaron explained what they had planned for Michi, Serena got the chills. She willed herself to remember the man's crimes.

When Stuart first asked if she wanted to go along, she flippantly declared that whatever he had planned for Michi wouldn't be bad enough.

Now she wasn't so sure.

Chapter 73
Bur Safaga, Egypt

Colette Logan slipped ashore after the others left the *Josie* with Ciro Michi. Using one of the jet skis, she made land and headed directly for the bus station where she booked a ticket for Cairo. The trip north gave her ample time to think. Thankfully, the night bus had few travelers on board.

For the first time in years, she didn't want to leave a job. Though they hadn't had much time for pleasantries, the team was companionable, determined and friendly.

But they didn't know her story—that she, too, was to blame.

She hoped her work to bring down Ciro Michi would compensate for the guilt. She hoped the nightmares would go away, and that she could start a new life. She didn't try to sleep on the bus. Michi's warning about his life insurance policy kept her on alert. She could still see the satisfied gleam in his eye and hear his heavily accented English. *If I die, whoever is responsible will be paid in full.*

Colette reached Cairo in the early morning and took a taxi from the bus station to El Qahira International Airport. She paid cash for a British Airways flight and settled herself in a café where she purchased Ethiopian coffee and a half hour of internet time.

Colette typed one last email to the senator. She wanted one more favor out of a man who knew she had enough dirt to bring him down. She wanted a name cleared.

Senator,

I require a favor: A clean slate for New York Times reporter, Zachary Morgan.

The man is innocent.

Sincerely,

Lakshanya Brookes.

Chapter 74
Theban Hills, near Luxor, Egypt

Kilo stopped the van. They got out and stood in the black Egyptian night marked by stars and the distant glow of Luxor. The sand reflected a white-faced moon, giving enough light to see.

"We need to work fast. None of us are looking forward to this part." He turned to Kilo and Aaron. "You ready?"

Long ago, but not far away, slaves chiseled burial chambers in the Theban hills for ancient pharaohs. Elaborate doorways carved in soft limestone cliffs marked these chambers. Over sixty pharaohs were buried in the Valley of the Kings between the 16th and 11th century, BC.

But the pharaohs weren't the only ones seeking immortality. Others with financial means purchased their own way into the afterlife. The Valley of the Kings was prime real estate. But here, in the adjacent valley at the knee wall of the Theban hills, slaves of the lesser-known wasted their lives carving smaller chambers. Student archaeologists spent semesters abroad studying these and posted findings on blogs devoted to the minor figures of Egypt's long history. Every student hoped to unearth the next great discovery. But permits to dig were difficult to procure and progress was slow under the hovering government minders. Often the discovery of an opening ended in nothing but an unmarked and relatively inconsequential shaft. Even the ancient Egyptians abandoned projects for lack of funds.

Stuart turned to Serena. "Start taking pictures. You're flash won't be noticed out here." He put a steadying hand on her shoulder. "Try not to think about what is happening. It will be over soon."

Stuart had already gone over the particulars. A photographer usually tried to incorporate the cultural and geographic elements of a place in order to give a sense of scope and context. This time she had to focus in on only one face. No other hands, feet or faces could show. Zachary's work, summarizing the charges and writing up a justification on the website would come later.

Sometime during the night Ciro Michi woke up inside the casket. His panic steadily increased, but they ignored his kicking. Aaron and Kilo pulled the casket out of the delivery van and opened the lid.

Michi scrambled up, blubbering with gratitude for being let out. His bound hands had turned a dull shade of purple from the zip tie. He had no recollection of leaving his yacht. Kilo cooked up a cocktail powerful enough to knock him out, but the effects of the drug had worn off and Ciro Michi would be awake the rest of the night.

Aaron and Kilo pulled him in front of the van headlights. Michi still wore a fine linen shirt over khaki pants. Though in his sixties, the man appeared to be in good health. His gratitude wore off and he started demanding explanations in Italian before switching to English.

"What are you doing with me? You have no right to keep me here. Take me back to my boat."

Stuart stepped up and looked directly into his face. "Mr. Michi, you are responsible for the death of over five million people along the Zambezi River."

"What are you talking about?" Michi spat. The man seemed to be recovering his arrogance but hadn't yet grasped the desperate nature of his position.

Stuart kept going. "You have enslaved thousands of people, forcing them to prostitute themselves for your own financial gain. According to my sources, you have personally trafficked over twenty-five thousand women in your lifetime." Stuart maintained a matter-of-fact tone. No emotion.

Michi began to fidget. His hands worked at his sides, looking for something to say. He glanced around, expecting to find the face of someone who would help.

"Michi, this is the end of the line for you. On behalf of the fathers whose children you have trafficked, I pronounce judgment against you. You are going to die. We will not, personally, hurt you. Instead, we will put you where you can't hurt anyone again."

"You are crazy." A quiver in Michi's voice belied his attempt at nonchalance.

"Show him." Stuart nodded to Kilo and Aaron. They walked Michi a few feet toward a boulder almost as large as a man. Serena and Zachary followed. It reminded Serena of the stone outside the Holy Sepulcher in Jerusalem. Beside the boulder, a door led into the face of the hill. Stuart turned on a flashlight, illuminating the cave.

"The hall is carved from stone," Stuart said. "This passageway will lead you to hell. It was the beginning of a tomb for an ancient Egyptian nobleman. Too good for you, but it will serve our purposes." He shone the flashlight directly into Michi's face, making the old man squint. "Ciro, have you ever been in absolute darkness? Your eyes can be wide open and still see nothing."

"My security people are already coming after you. They will find you." Michi tried to sound convincing.

"Perhaps." Stuart shrugged, "But they will never find you."

"You are a fool." Michi's attempt to keep up his bravado started to crumble. The man's body began to shiver. It was a cold Michi had never known before.

Stuart continued. "You will be given no food or water. If you are lucky, you will live three days. Your hands and feet will be bound and the entrance sealed by that great stone."

"And you are just going to leave me there?" A new kind of horror

187

began to dawn on Michi. He fought to keep teeth from chattering as he spoke. "You cannot just leave me here alone."

"I am not going leave you here by yourself. That wouldn't be nice." He turned to Kilo. "Show him his company."

Kilo brought over a Plexiglas container. Stuart grabbed Michi by his shirt and pulled him close to the glass before shining the flashlight inside, so he could see. Small yellow and brown scorpions swarmed under the beam of light.

Michi's eyes grew wide; he tried to pull himself back from the creatures, but Stuart grabbed a fistful of Michi's hair and pressed his face up against the glass. "Get a good look, Michi. I want you to remember what they look like, before it gets too dark to see."

In spite of himself, Ciro Michi could not take his eyes off the mass of yellowish scorpions.

Stuart returned to his lesson on the arachnids. "These are not just any scorpions. They are called the deathstalker. A gift from a friend of mine. Not many around these parts, but they are special."

"Let me go. I can make you a rich man. I have gold." Ciro started to beg and Serena's camera captured growing terror on the man's face.

"The gold?" Stuart paused. "We know about that. Colette checked out the pallets from Italy. It will help the countries you ruined put themselves together."

"Stop. I have a family." Ciro Michi pleaded.

Stuart continued, unmoved. "The deathstalker is one of the few scorpions whose bite is fatal. Perhaps, if you stay still, they might not sting. However, when you panic in the dark and start to lose your mind, they will sting. I've heard it is quite painful. The neurotoxins eventually cause pulmonary edema."

"Please." Michi dropped to his knees. Kilo and Aaron stretched him out and pulled off his shoes and socks. Aaron held him down while Kilo bound his feet with a single zip tie.

Stuart kept talking. "I'm not a doctor; but I think it will feel like drowning. First, a tightening in your chest. Then, you will breathe but not be able to get your breath because fluid will slowly accumulate in your lungs."

Michi started to sob like a child, frequently switching from Italian to English. Several times he started reciting the Lord's Prayer in Latin but never finished.

"Take him in," Stuart said.

Ciro Michi went berserk. He thrashed and bit at the men who carried him into the tunnel. Serena forced herself to take photos, and remember the man's crimes.

One small, old man struggling violently against the three. Obscene shadows stretched on chiseled walls around them, their voices muted by rock.

At the far end of the hall they dropped him on the floor next to a stone sarcophagus. The rectangle had been part of the original stone, emerging from the floor as they carved around it. Its heavy stone lid had already been pushed back. Suddenly the man stopped screaming and began speaking gibberish. Serena and Zachary stood at the entrance listening to the bizarre and illogical sequence of words interspersed with childish laughter. Aaron exited the passageway and returned with the arachnids. Michi knelt awkwardly, squinting in the light and saw them, too.

He stopped jabbering and sobbing and smiled sweetly. "Please, no?" Two, pathetic, coherent words. The voice of a little boy in an old man.

They lifted a strangely pliant Michi into the stone vault. Stuart set the Plexiglas container next to him and removed the lid.

Stuart replied. "Ciro Michi. Your actions have condemned you. There is only one way out. Make your peace with God."

Serena's camera shutter clicked in rapid succession as Aaron and Stuart wedged their backs against the wall and put their feet stone lid. At last it thumped into place, pinching out the last of Michi's scream.

The men exited the chamber. Kilo had the delivery van's crash bar in position to push the stone over the entrance. The engine revved and the stone, grinding against the metal bumper slid across the opening.

Serena snapped a few more pictures. Just the rock. No horizon lines. No faces. The camera shook in her hands.

Stuart gently touched her shoulder. His face was grim. "Always remember, because of what we have done here, this man will never again steal people from their villages. He will never be able to force them into sexual slavery for his own profit. He will pay for the five million lives he erased for his own greed."

In spite of herself, tears began to fall from Serena's eyes. "I'm sorry." She shrugged, embarrassed.

Stuart held her like a father holds his daughter.

The other men stood by. Stuart pulled a silver flask from his pocket. "Take a drink, luv. It will help calm your nerves."

She took a hit and they passed it around.

Chapter 75
Off the East Coast of Africa

The *Josie* rounded the Somali Peninsula and tracked south-east through the Indian Ocean toward the island of Mauritius 700 miles west of Madagascar. They had ample fuel supply and the weather cooperated to make for calm seas. Aaron Ball assured them the boat could almost run by itself, but he spent several hours a day teaching Zachary the finer details of operation and navigation. Even Zachary had to admit it was pretty simple. The intuitive controls looked intimidating, but the incorporation of the latest in high-end marine GPS systems took most of the guesswork out of it.

Under Stuart's direction the reporters completed their work by the time they had left the Gulf of Aden. Stuart wanted the job done so they could move on. The files would be taken to Zimbabwe for Chuma to upload to the web site.

Zachary and Serena also prepared a story for Serena's agent, Jarret Miller. The man would find the best venue for its release and ensure the actual source of the story remained a secret.

Zachary and Serena wrapped up their work on the computer, and tried to unwind.

"Let's get some sun," Zachary suggested. He put his hands gently on her shoulders, massaging the tension that had been there since the tomb. At Stuart's insistence, Serena and Zachary were billeted in a suite. Zachary led the way through the lounge and sliding glass doors to a private balcony that faced the stern. The Indian Ocean stretched as far as they could see.

"It is so beautiful." Serena slipped her arm around Zachary. "I wish it could last forever."

"Me, too." He turned and looked at Serena. "I've been waiting for a time like this." Zachary shifted his eyes, looking out at sea again. "But it seems to get harder the longer I wait." He dug in his pocket.

"I want this to last forever, too. Not the boat or the sea, but being with you." He pulled out the ring and got down on one knee. Serena bit her bottom lip, suddenly realizing what he was doing.

"Serena. I have no house, no job and I'm a wanted man in the places I call home. All I have to offer is myself. And I'll give you that, forever if you'll marry me." The last bit seemed to get stuck in his throat.

Serena stood smiling and laughing, tears rolling off her cheeks.

"Is that a 'yes'?" Zachary asked.

Serena wrapped her arms around his neck and whispered in his ear, "It's a yes."

A cheer erupted behind them. Stuart, Aaron and Kilo had all sneaked up to their deck, champagne in hand with extras for the newly-engaged.

"I was starting to wonder if you'd ever get around to it," Aaron said. "If you hadn't hurried up, I might have taken a shot myself."

They laughed.

"A toast," Stuart announced. They lifted their glasses, "To the mystery of love."

It was the best champagne Ciro Michi had to offer.

Other books by this author include:

The Zambezi Chronicles
    The Contract*
    Critical Fault*
    Cover of Darkness

And

The Moderator Series
    The Moderator
    The Coma
    Grid Lock**

*Now available in audio from Audible.com.

**Release February 2014

On Facebook at www.facebook.com/dwightkoppbooks

On the web at www.dwightkopp.com .

Acknowledgments

I am thankful for the editing assistance of Doe Kopp, Martha Squaresky and Jay Squaresky. My book is better because of their input.

Any remaining errors are, of course, entirely my fault.

About the Author

Dwight Kopp lived (mostly) in Zambia until he was thirteen. His fondest memories include listening to the sound of elephants raiding the peanut fields as he drifted off to sleep.

He now lives and writes in Lancaster County where he married the woman of his dreams. They have five (amazing) children.